Her bridges burned behind her, Erin walked silently and steadily until she stood in the open doorway. "Keith?"

He turned slowly. Her bright hair was gleaming and tousled around her face, and she was dressed for bed. Dressed for him.

Suddenly he was standing before her, his hands lifting to her shoulders. He didn't think he'd be able to let go of her this time. "Are you sure?" he demanded, his voice harsh.

She didn't flinch from the sound, but wrapped her arms around his neck. "I'm sure." It was hardly more than a whisper, and Keith had no will left to ask again. It felt as if something had broken inside him, some restraining wall around the desire that had smoldered there since he'd first heard her speak. He bent slightly from the waist, both his arms wrapping around her, and when he straightened he had lifted her completely off her feet.

Erin heard—felt—a pounding, but didn't know if it was her heart or his. Wrapped in his powerful arms and almost crushed against his chest, she felt so surrounded by him that they might have had only one heart between them. . . .

WHAT ARE *LOVESWEPT* ROMANCES?

They are stories of true romance and touching emotion. We believe those two very important ingredients are constants in our highly sensual and very believable stories in the *LOVESWEPT* line. Our goal is to give you, the reader, stories of consistently high quality that may sometimes make you laugh, sometimes make you cry, but are always fresh and creative and contain many delightful surprises within their pages.

Most romance fans read an enormous number of books. Those they truly love, they keep. Others may be traded with friends and soon forgotten. We hope that each *LOVESWEPT* romance will be a treasure—a "keeper." We will always try to publish

*LOVE STORIES YOU'LL NEVER FORGET
BY AUTHORS YOU'LL ALWAYS REMEMBER*

The Editors

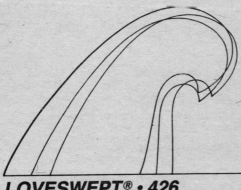

LOVESWEPT® • 426

Kay Hooper
The Lady and the Lion

 BANTAM BOOKS
NEW YORK • TORONTO • LONDON • SYDNEY • AUCKLAND

THE LADY AND THE LION
A Bantam Book / October 1990

If you would be interested in receiving protective vinyl
covers for your Loveswept books, please write to this
address for information:

Loveswept
Bantam Books
P. O. Box 985
Hicksville, NY 11802

ISBN 0-553-44057-8

Published simultaneously in the United States and Canada

Bantam Books are published by Bantam Books, a division
of Bantam Doubleday Dell Publishing Group, Inc. Its trademark, consisting of the words "Bantam Books" and the
portrayal of a rooster, is Registered in U.S. Patent and
Trademark Office and in other countries. Marca Regis-
trada. Bantam Books, 666 Fifth Avenue, New York, New
York 10103.

PRINTED IN THE UNITED STATES OF AMERICA

OPM   0 9 8 7 6 5 4 3 2 1

Death is afraid of him
because he has the heart of a lion.

—ARAB PROVERB

Author's Note

Fiction is rife with stories of people forced to live a half life for one reason or another. In the fairy tale whose title I have borrowed, a prince was forced to exist as a lion during the day, and walked as a man only at night. Of course, we don't believe in curses, do we?

But suppose a man shaped his own curse. Suppose that he was compelled to live differently by day and by night because only by doing so could he attain a specific goal. By night, he lives in a dangerous world; by day, he can be himself.

Or . . . can he?

Prologue

"Who is he?"

"Says his name's Duncan. Claims to represent a cartel operating out of Colombia."

"What do you think?"

"His boat's Colombian registry; so's the jet. He spends money like water, and throws parties almost every night. He has the locals eating out of his hand."

"Drug money?"

"Looks that way."

Guy Wellman drummed his fingers against the desk, frowning. He was a middle-aged man, in good shape, with distinguished gray hair and a self-satisfied expression stamped into his heavy features. That smug expression had eroded over the past months, so that now he seemed more petulant than impressive.

His assistant, a quiet man with a hard face and shuttered eyes, watched his boss unemotionally.

"And he wants to meet me?" Wellman asked finally.

"Says he has a business proposition for you."

"I don't touch drugs," Wellman said emphatically.

"I gather he knows that. My bet is that he wants to smooth the way for his cartel. He said he needed a man of influence and respectability to deal 'properly' with officials."

Wellman scowled. "That bastard Arturo's already using me—why should I ask this one to do the same?"

After an almost imperceptible hesitation, his assistant said, "If his cartel is as powerful as he says, it wouldn't hurt to listen to the proposition."

"All right, all right. Arrange a meeting."

One

The clock on her nightstand softly chimed the hour as Erin Prentice hung up the phone, but she didn't need to glance at it. Five A.M., ten A.M. in London. It was the best time to catch her father—just after breakfast and before his full schedule of morning meetings. After so many years, she knew his schedule, often to the minute. And though he hadn't asked it of her, she had automatically suited her schedule to his.

Ironic, she thought. She wasn't supposed to *be* on a schedule; that was the point of this vacation. One of them, anyway. But habit died hard. By placing the call at this hour on her first morning in Miami Beach, she had tacitly agreed to call him every morning at the same time, and he would expect her to continue to do so.

Restless, Erin rose from the chair by her phone and went out into her sitting room, absently tightening the belt of her robe. She opened the French doors leading onto her balcony, and stepped out into the coolness of the predawn quiet that was broken only by the pounding of the waves. The balcony overlooked Miami's famous expanse of white beach. First light was seeping in the east, beginning to separate the horizon into sky and ocean.

It was peaceful. She could see that, but couldn't feel it herself. What she felt was frustration, guilt, and a grinding uncertainty about the direction her future should take. But above all, she felt isolated.

The realization had barely crossed her mind when Erin heard a soft sound, the creak of a chaise as weight was shifted slightly. She looked quickly to the right, the first stab of unease fading as she remembered what the desk clerk had told her. Her suite connected to the one next to it, big double doors between the rooms could be opened if a guest wanted a much larger suite. Now the balcony was shared, so a stout latticework screen fashioned of steel strips was bolted firmly in place in the center to provide privacy to both occupants of the suites. For good measure, there were additional folding screens on either side of the divider to be used if even more privacy was needed.

The latticework of the steel screen was closely woven, so that Erin could see nothing at first. Then a faint red glow became briefly visible, and an elusive aroma of tobacco told her that her neighbor was smoking. Erin hesitated, wary of speaking to a stranger, but both her background and her overwhelming sense of isolation drove her to acknowledge the presence of someone else.

"It's beautiful, isn't it?" she said, resting her hands on the waist-high masonry wall and turning her attention back toward the shimmering grayness of the sea and sky.

After a moment, a man responded, "Very beautiful. Very peaceful." His voice was deep and low, with a slight hint of restraint or tension.

Erin unconsciously tilted her head a bit as she listened to the voice rather than the words. In her father's world, where gamesmanship was subtle and careful, she had learned to pay more attention to tone and nuance, to all the things never spelled out in words. It was second nature to her to do so.

And what she heard in this man's voice intrigued her. The tension, she thought, seemed more physical than emotional, as if he were too tired or too edgy to relax. There was strength in his voice as well, power, a kind of certainty that told her he was very sure of his place in the world around him. Erin wanted to hear more, wanted to define the other things she heard, the shades and shadows and undercurrents. She forgot about merely being polite and courteous.

"I've always been an early riser," she said, keeping her own voice carefully neutral. "You too?"

As before, a moment passed before he answered. "I work nights. This is the end of a day for me."

Which explained the tension, Erin decided. He hadn't yet wound down enough to rest. She wanted to ask what his job was, thinking with mild curiosity that it must be temporary work of some kind since he was staying in a hotel, but she didn't want to seem too nosy. "I'm on vacation," she offered, still gazing out at the dark ocean. "And even now I can't make myself sleep late."

"Habits are difficult to break." His voice was a shade more relaxed now, but still slow and measured, reminding her of the tone her father used when he was talking to someone he hadn't quite made up his mind about.

She nodded, even though she knew he couldn't

see her as anything more than a shadow. "Habits. Schedules. Sometimes I think the worst thing mankind ever did was invent a way of measuring time. We've become slaves to clocks." Listening to herself, Erin had to laugh. "Sorry. Dawn brings out the worst in me."

"It's a time of transition," the man said quietly. "It doesn't exist in itself except as a few minutes between night and day, a time when we ask ourselves the tough questions."

She thought he had probably asked himself a lot of tough questions. It was in his voice, something subtle she had heard only in the voices of highly intelligent, very powerful men. It was the sound of an intense inner drive that wasn't ambition for its own sake but rather a profound desire to accomplish something of importance.

"But when do the answers come?" she murmured.

"Another dawn. If we're lucky."

Still listening more to his voice than the words, Erin deliberately lightened the subject. "I'm not so sure I believe in luck. I always lose at card games. Now is that bad luck or just an inability to play cards?"

"Is your memory good?" he asked.

"Very good."

A thread of amusement entered his voice. "Then you're simply not paying attention to the cards. Skill at card games is almost entirely a matter of concentration."

"I do tend to let my mind wander," she admitted, smiling as she watched the sky lighten. "Winning a card game never seemed very important."

"Not unless you bet the kingdom," he said.

She laughed softly. "I never bet more than I can afford to lose."

"Wise of you."

Dawn was, as he'd observed, minutes only; light was gaining strength. Erin felt a sudden and peculiarly vivid regret at losing the anonymity of darkness. As brief as this time had been, she felt more at peace now. And, perhaps oddly, she had no inclination to see the face of her neighbor, or ask his name. It was pleasant, the lack of any demand in the faceless, nameless conversation, and she felt no need to change their relationship.

In her experience, knowledge brought demands between people, and that was the last thing she wanted right now.

Trying to keep the regret out of her voice, she said, "I should let you rest. Besides, another habit of mine is running every morning."

"You should be careful," he said. "This isn't the safest part of the world."

She could have told him that she had taken her daily run in places where soldiers patrolled. Where, in fact, wars had raged outside carefully marked and guarded neutral ground. But what she said was, "Thanks, I will. It's been nice talking to you."

"Likewise."

Erin retreated from the balcony, closing the French doors and automatically locking them. She went to change into her sweatsuit, glancing, this time, at the double doors leading into the other suite; the doors were securely locked, of course.

Her father would have told her she'd been foolish in talking to a strange man, in telling him she ran every morning on the beach. She wondered why she'd done it. Not that it mattered. She had a feeling her neighbor was as disinclined to meet her as she was to meet him, so he was unlikely to pursue a friendship.

Changing into her sweatsuit and running shoes, Erin amused herself by imagining the most likely—or unlikely—face and personality for her quiet neighbor. He was probably on the shady side of fifty, she decided, and his "work" was some high-stakes poker game played in a dark and smoke-filled room somewhere.

The talk of card games must have put that into her head, she realized.

He'd left a wife and kiddies back in Topeka while he followed some obscure poker circuit, winning and losing fortunes over the years. . . .

Erin frowned slightly, pulled from the fantasy by the instincts that were telling her she was way off base. There had been too much strength in his voice to allow for the transient, risky life of a gambler, too much depth to permit him to be anything so trivial.

She glanced at the big double doors again as she passed through the sitting room on her way out, and ruthlessly ignored her growing curiosity. Absurd. Her own isolation was putting ridiculous ideas into her head, making her speculate without any good reason. Her neighbor was just a man, that was all, a man who had talked to her for a few quiet moments on a dark balcony.

She took her key and left the suite, determinedly ignoring the door just down the hall as she headed for the elevator. But she noticed the Do Not Disturb sign he'd hung out. Symbolic, she decided. He didn't want to be disturbed—and neither did she.

As the slender young woman took the walkway to the beach and broke into an easy jog, a very old man stepped from the shadows near a cabana and watched her. The first rays of the morning sun touched him, illuminating his white suit and his thick, snowy hair and beard in a way that seemed just a bit unreal. He propped elegant hands on a gold-headed cane, the pose suggesting thoughtfulness rather than infirmity.

After a few moments, he turned his head and looked upward, his dark, benign gaze searching until it located a particular balcony a dozen floors up. There was a figure up there that might have been a man, his attention fixed on the beach and the young woman taking her morning run.

The old man watched the younger for some time, his stillness complete, dark eyes very intent. It was as if he were listening to some soft, far-off voice that demanded his utmost attention. Then, imperceptibly, he relaxed, and a singularly sweet smile curved his lips.

"Now then," he said in a rich, gentle baritone, nodding slightly to himself. "Now then, we'll see."

Keith Donovan leaned his forearms on the balcony wall and watched the lone figure running along the beach. He was too far away to have a clear look at her. All he could be certain about was how slender she was and how long her red hair was.

And an incredible voice. A slight accent, very faint—more cosmopolitan, he thought, than anything else. But that voice . . . musical and oddly haunting, unusually expressive, it had pulled at him in a way he'd never felt before.

He told himself he was just tired. The past months had left him feeling so disconnected that a sweet voice on a dark balcony had seemed a lifeline. That was it. That was why her voice had affected him this way.

It wasn't a reassuring thought. He couldn't afford any distractions, couldn't spare the emotional energy for—for what? Keith frowned, his gaze still on the tiny figure now almost out of sight. What was he worried about? She certainly hadn't indicated that he was anything more than a neighbor she had spoken to out of politeness. The conversation had been brief, and she had neither offered her name nor asked to know his.

So why did he feel so affected by her? The question was troubling, and Keith brushed it away almost violently. He forced himself to turn away, to retreat inside his room and firmly close the balcony doors. With a long, tense night behind him, he needed sleep, but he had discovered it was difficult for him to wind down, to drop his guard and rest. That was why he'd developed the habit of sitting out on his balcony and watching the dawn each morning, needing the interlude of peace.

The conversation with the woman had helped him to relax, he knew, but he didn't like it. Still, having learned to take what came, he blanked his mind and went to bed.

It was afternoon when he rose, and he quite deliberately avoided going out onto his balcony even though his curiosity about the woman had increased. He ordered room service, remaining in his suite because that, too, was habit, cautious habit. Careful, wary habit. The fewer people who saw him, the less chance there was of the wrong person seeing him in the wrong place and out of character.

But today, for the first time, he was edgy, restless. He left the suite only once, going to the hotel's gym to work out as he sometimes did, needing the exercise but, even more, needing an outlet for tension and excess energy. Today, it didn't seem to help much. The hours between waking and leaving to go to the boat seemed to stretch forever, and it was a relief when he finally left his suite just after eight that evening. As usual, he took the stairs and left the hotel unobtrusively by a side exit.

He changed between hotel and boat: He changed his clothes and hair, his posture, his voice. He pushed from his mind a quiet hotel suite, a darkened balcony, a soft voice, and peace. When he stepped onto the boat, he was someone else. Someone whose laugh held a reckless, ruthless, dangerous edge.

It was after four the next morning when he returned to his silent hotel suite. He showered, washing away the clinging scents of cheap perfume, smoke, and liquor, then wrapped a towel around his waist and went out onto the dark balcony. He was as weary as usual, yet this morning was different and he was conscious of the difference only after he'd settled into the chaise.

He was listening, he realized. He was waiting for the soft click of French doors opening on the other side of the security screen, for the whisper of silk as she moved. He had heard both the morning before, despite the muted roar of the waves far below, and he was listening for the sounds now.

Keith shook his head slightly. This was absurd, he told himself. And dangerous. He'd chosen, eyes wide open, to stand alone in this, and he had no right forming even a transient relationship with anyone who wasn't involved in what he was doing.

He stared out at the dark ocean, telling himself to go back inside, to simply cut the tenuous connection before it could become something too important to lose. But even as the wary voice inside him murmured that warning, he couldn't help but question it. What was he risking, after all? A few minutes of dawn peace shared with a stranger. And besides, she probably wouldn't even come out again.

The thought had barely registered when he heard the soft click of her balcony doors, the whisper of silk as she moved. He felt her presence on the other side of the screen with an intensity that took him by surprise, and he couldn't stop himself from greeting her.

"Good morning."

"Good morning."

She was disturbed, he realized instantly; it was in her voice, a tremor that could have been pain or anger—or both. He found himself turning slightly toward the screen, staring at it as if he could penetrate it and the darkness. But he couldn't, of course, not with his eyes.

"Bad night?" he asked quietly.

A kind of laugh reached his ears, a sound that held very little humor. "No, the night was all right."

He was silent for a moment, then spoke in the same quiet, undemanding tone. "Sometimes, it's easier to talk to a stranger when we're upset. And easier to be honest in the darkness."

"Dawn questions?"

"Only if you want me to ask them," he told her. "I'll listen, if you do. Maybe the answers will come."

If she hesitated, it was momentary, and when she spoke again her voice was taut. "How do you tell someone you love that you can't be what he wants you to be?"

Keith felt a strange pang that he refused to acknowledge. "What does he want you to be?

"There." She laughed, again with no humor. "Just there, on the edge of his life. Playing the role he wants me to play. Shaping my life to fit his."

"And you can't do that?"

"I have. For a long time. And it's . . . smothering me. The demands and expectations. It wouldn't be so bad if I felt useful, that I mattered. But all his attention is devoted to his work, and sometimes I think I'm invisible to him. I have to break away. At least, I think I do. But I don't know how to tell him without hurting him. And I don't know what I'll do after."

"What do you want to do?" Keith asked.

She sighed. "I don't know. That's one reason I'm here, to try and figure it out. And now . . . This morning, when I called, he told me to come home. Back to London. He can't find anything, he said, and his secretary is hopeless. He needs me to keep his life running smoothly."

"That doesn't make you feel that you matter to him?"

"No. Someone else could do what I do. It isn't *me* he values, it's what I do for him."

Keith hesitated, then repeated, "What do you want to do?"

"I don't want to go back. Not yet. It's such a strong habit, to be what he expects, that I'm afraid I'll just take the path of least resistance if I go back now."

He couldn't help but wonder, with another

strange and unacknowledged pang, if they were discussing her husband or lover. It sounded that way, he thought. He didn't want to ask outright, wary of being something other than the disinterested and impersonal voice he had promised to be. So he kept his voice soft, his questions dispassionate.

"Did you tell him?"

"No. I told him I was enjoying my vacation, told him I need the break."

"Why can't you tell him the truth?"

"I don't want to hurt him."

"You're hurting yourself by remaining silent. Wouldn't *that* hurt him if he knew?"

"I don't know."

She sounded a little lost now, and he responded instinctively to that pain. "You aren't sure he loves you?"

"No, I'm sure he does. It's just . . . well, his career is the most important thing in his life. I think he expects it to be the most important thing in *my* life too. You see, I'm something of an asset to his career. He's told me that more than once. Others have told me as well."

Keith was too curious to let that pass. "How are you an asset?" he asked. For a long moment, it seemed as though she wouldn't answer, but then she did, her voice holding a hint of constraint.

"It's difficult to explain. There were people he was having trouble making connections with until I began to act as his hostess at dinners and parties. People would tell me things they wouldn't tell him, things he needed to know. He says I have the knack of listening."

Frowning in the darkness, Keith said, "He's using you." There was a slight sound on the other

side of the screen, as if she moved almost instinctively in protest.

"It didn't seem so at first. Meeting people, talking to them. I never got information damaging to
anyone, just little things, bits and pieces that
might have given him an edge. I was willing to
do it. It's important, what he does, and I agree
with his goals. Usually."

"But not always." It wasn't a question.

"No. No, not always." Her voice turned rueful.
"But he says that I don't understand the large
picture, the long-term view of things. That my
duty is to tell him whatever I learn and let him
decide what's to be done with the knowledge."

"How do you feel about that?" Keith asked.

"Patronized." The response was instant and
sharp. After a moment, she laughed a bit shakily.
"It all began to build up inside me, that's why I
left." She hesitated again, then said, "I'm sorry. I
have no right to dump all this in your lap."

Keith, who had been thinking even as he listened, ignored her words. Slowly, he said, "Someone you love expects you to play a part that makes
you uncomfortable, to be a pipeline for information that helps him in his career. He expects you
to fit yourself into his life in a way that satisfies
his needs rather than yours. You feel you don't
matter to him except in that role. Even more, his
demands are smothering you. Your own thoughts
and opinions aren't valued, your life isn't yours
to live."

"Did I say all that?" Her voice was small.

"I think you did."

"I'm sorry."

Turning his gaze out toward the ocean and the
graying darkness that heralded daybreak, Keith
said, "Don't be. I'm just here to listen to the tough

member? And the most im-
think, is—what are you going
problem? Running away hasn't
g."

t you did. You couldn't tell him how
you   so you just left. But now he wants you
to come home. so what are you going to do?"

"I'm not going home. Not yet. Maybe if I stay
away long enough . . . "

"He'll change? Do you really believe what you're
saying?"

"No." She sighed almost inaudibly. "I don't. He
doesn't even recognize a problem. And he won't
until I confront him. That's what you're saying,
isn't it?"

"You said it."

"I'll hurt him. I don't want to hurt him."

Keith hesitated, then said, "Do you really believe
it's better to go on hurting yourself? To go on
living a life you don't want, being a person you're
not? If he knew what this was doing to you, do
you believe he'd choose to enrich his life at the
expense of yours?"

Answering the last question, she said very quietly, "I hope not."

They were both silent for several minutes while
the sky lightened in the east, and then she stirred
slightly. "Tough questions. It doesn't help much
that I know the answers."

"Sometimes," he said, "knowing the answers
gives you nothing except more questions."

"Until another dawn?" Her voice was wistful.

He hesitated, then said, "Don't force it. Take
the time you need and let the answers sort themselves out. We always know what's best for us, if

we'll just be patient and allow our instincts to tell us."

"Then I'll try. Thanks. I had no right to impose, but you've been a lot of help."

"No problem." He resisted the urge to keep the conversation going, telling himself firmly there wouldn't be any more morning interludes like this one. Already, he'd gotten involved despite himself, her problems worrying him, and he just didn't have the energy to spare. It had to stop.

"Well . . . thanks again," she murmured, and he listened in silence to the soft sounds of her leaving the balcony.

He sat gazing out at the dawn, watching the first reddening of the horizon become a blazing sunrise. He did get up and look down on the beach where she was beginning her morning run. Red hair. Beyond that, he didn't think very much. After a while, he went into his suite and to bed.

He didn't go out onto his balcony the next morning.

Erin spent most of the day just thinking. She walked on the beach, swam in the hotel's pool, treated herself to a sauna and massage. It was rare for her, this luxury of time to herself, and she enjoyed it. The sense of guilt she felt at so abruptly having deserted her father was still with her, but fainter now and much less painful than it had been.

Other problems didn't seem so overwhelming now, and she was even able to feel a kind of wry amusement at the number of male hotel guests who apparently felt she shouldn't be alone. It was something Erin had coped with since her teens, and the stage of being flattered by the attention was long past. She had learned, often painfully, that her looks drew men who were never interested in seeing beneath the centerfold proportions and striking features . . . men who never cared about her ideas or her feelings.

But they did want to talk to her. Oh, yes. They talked as if a dam had burst. They spilled out words in a torrent tending to stare at her while doing so, telling her things she had no right to know. That was the "asset" her father appreciated so much. Even men with high security clearances who certainly should have known better told her things they shouldn't.

To impress her, according to her father.

Her quiet balcony-neighbor had been right; her father was using her to further his own ambitions. Perhaps she'd feel differently about her talent if it were important in her own career or project to be able to glean information—but she doubted it. Seldom willing to hide her own motives or intelligence for any reason, she was unlikely to choose a career that demanded an ability to interrogate or dissemble.

So what *did* she want to do with her life? A tricky question—especially for a woman of twenty-eight who should have made her choice long ago.

The answer came to her that night as she lay awake in bed, drifted into her mind and settled firmly. She wanted a simple life. Love, a home, children.

She had grown up in a lifestyle so many people seemed to think was glamorous. The expensive schools, living and vacationing in exotic places, wealth. She had worn jewels and designer gowns, sailed on yachts, flown in private jets. She had, quite literally, danced with princes.

But she had never felt she quite belonged in that life. More comfortable with her hair loose and her face free of makeup, wearing jeans or sweatpants, she had turned herself into a part-time lady to please her father. Now, lying awake in her quiet bedroom, she knew it had been a loving gesture that had backfired. She could be a part-time lady, but she could never replace her mother and she couldn't go on submerging so much of herself out of guilt.

She wanted a home and family. She wanted a simple life. She wanted to paint.

That last was so surprising a thought that she actually caught her breath. Paint? Well, sure, she'd painted in school; in fact, her art teacher had said she was quite good. But she'd never been conscious of the desire to go on with it. Had she?

Erin let the tantalizing thought follow her into sleep, quite wary of making a quick—and possibly wrong—choice.

She woke up around four and ordered coffee and juice sent up, grateful for twenty-four-hour room service that delivered her order promptly. It helped her to be awake and clear-minded when she called London a few minutes later. The call went through quickly, and she kept her voice calm and casual when she greeted her father.

"Hi, Dad." Characteristically, her father had more important things on his mind than a polite greeting.

"Erin, I can't find next month's schedule. Where on earth did you put it?"

"It's in the center drawer of your desk." she answered automatically. "Dad—"

"They want me in Turkey in six weeks. Burleigh's retiring, and I'm to fill the post for at least a year. It means packing up and moving again, but there shouldn't be a problem, you've gotten quite good at it. The residence is furnished, of course—"

"Dad." Erin drew a deep breath. "I won't be going with you, to Turkey or anywhere else."

"Nonsense, of course you will." Richard Fane Prentice, Earl of Westford and the ambassador Britain chose to utilize for temporary duty in sensitive areas of the globe, sounded merely impatient. "There's a great deal to do, Erin, so you'd better come home right away."

"No," she said softly.

Silence, utter and astounded, greeted that simple word.

Erin took another breath. "Dad, I didn't choose a diplomatic career. You did. It's your life we're talking about, not mine. I have to live my life. I'm not even sure I want to stay in England. I've always felt more at home in the States." She hesitated. "I'm a coward to tell you like this, I know, but I just didn't know how to say it. I don't want to hurt you, or disappoint you, and I don't want us to fight—"

"Erin, what are you talking about?"

She winced at the grimness she heard in his voice, and forced herself not to weaken. "I'm talking about choices. I have to make my own, Dad. I have a lot of thinking to do, but I know that the one choice I won't make is to fit myself into your life because that's where you want me to be. I'm sorry."

"Come home," he said quietly. "We obviously need to talk, and not like this."

She managed a faint laugh. "No, I'm not brave enough to come home just yet. The habit of doing what you want is too strong. Besides, I know you'll ask questions—and I don't have all the answers. I will, but I need time to myself to find them."

"Erin, we have to talk about this."

"Yes. But not just now. I only wanted to tell you that I won't be coming home today—or in two weeks. I'm going to stay here for a while. Maybe go up to New England and visit Mother's family. And I won't be calling every morning. Your secretary isn't hopeless, Dad, and you aren't nearly as absent-minded as you think; you don't need me to keep your life in order."

He was silent.

There was a great deal Erin would have to tell him eventually. As he'd said, they needed to talk face to face. But even though she'd managed to say more than she had expected to be able to, she wasn't yet ready to confront the problems head-on. She'd given him something to think about, and that was enough for now.

"I'll call you in a few days."

"Erin—"

"In a few days, Dad. I love you. Bye." She cradled the receiver and stared at the phone for a few moments, feeling that a weight had eased even if it hadn't completely disappeared. She wasn't sure her father would patiently wait until she decided to call him again, but she hoped he would. And she brushed aside the faint pang of guilt she felt at having hit him with this just when he was preparing to take on a new assignment. Where her father was concerned, there would never be a "right" time, she knew.

She rose from the edge of the bed before she realized where she was going, but wasn't very surprised that her steps led her directly to the balcony doors. *He* had given her the courage to begin confronting her problems, and she wanted to tell him that. She opened the French doors and went out into the cool darkness.

He wasn't there. She knew. She felt it. There was an absence, an emptiness on the other side of the security screen. Still, distrusting her own senses, she couldn't help but ask softly, "Are you there?"

Silence, except for the muted sound of the waves below.

Disappointment and an odd sense of hurt swept over her, and Erin chided herself for the feelings. What was wrong with her? It wasn't as if they had an appointment out here, or that she could expect anything at all from him.

"Idiot," she muttered to herself. Maybe he'd gone straight to bed, tired after work. Or maybe his job had ended and he'd checked out of the hotel.

He was a stranger, after all. Just a quiet voice in the darkness that had eased her anxiety and shown her the right path to take. She didn't know him. Not his name. Not even what he looked like. And why did he matter to her? It was ridiculous. She'd *wanted* no demands, no obligations or expectations, and here she was upset because he wasn't where she'd expected him to be, where she wanted him to be.

She reminded herself of all that. But she waited. The eastern horizon lightened, graying toward dawn. The first purple and pink tendrils of light turned red and then gold. The sun peeked over the rim of the ocean cautiously, then lifted, finally, to announce a new day.

He didn't come.

Two

Keith hadn't expected it to be so difficult. He'd told himself firmly he wouldn't go out onto the balcony the third morning, and he managed not to. Instead, he had remained in his sitting room, gazing at the balcony doors, watching the dawn from that silent, lonely vantage point. When he finally went to bed, he didn't sleep well.

His first clear thought on waking in the afternoon was of her. He wondered if she'd called the man in her life, if she was still worried. He wanted to know those answers with an anxiety that unnerved him—and made him angry. What on earth was wrong with him? For months, he'd been single-minded to the point of obsession, all his thoughts and determination, all his emotions, fixed immovably on the plans he had so cautiously put into motion.

And now . . . He was so close he could almost feel hot breath on the back of his neck, the end of it all finally in sight, and at the very point when he most needed every thread of his concentration he couldn't get this woman out of his mind.

Dangerous wasn't the word for it.

He didn't know what it meant, this fixation on a woman whose name he didn't know, whose face he'd never seen. The timing couldn't have been worse, he didn't like what was happening to him. He didn't like it because he couldn't seem to control it.

Keith left the hotel earlier than usual and went to the marina, becoming that other man because *he* was untroubled by a sweet voice on a dark balcony, by unfamiliar feelings and troubling thoughts. The man who called himself Duncan wore his expensive silk suits, diamond rings, and Rolex™ with careless assurance and laughed often, though his eyes remained hard and enigmatic. Duncan owned a boat named *Ladama* and a Lear jet, both with Colombian registry. Almost every night he threw a party on his boat, one glittering affair after another where only the best food and wine were served.

But no drugs. Duncan had told Guy Wellman, a wealthy and powerful businessman who'd attended last night's party, that it wasn't wise for a man such as himself to let it be known he had access to drugs. Not wise at all. There was no need to advertise the fact and invite inconvenient attention from the law, he'd said with a laugh.

On this evening, at a small, rented apartment halfway between his hotel and the boat, Keith became Duncan, slipping into the skin of his alter ego with the ease of nightly practice, and thoroughly submerging his own personality. He moved among his guests when they arrived at the boat, expertly nursing one drink while giving the appearance of drinking a great deal, talking to everyone without saying anything of importance, his reckless laugh heard often. As the night wore on he became, outwardly, even more careless, betting and losing ten thousand dollars on a single throw of a pair of undoubtedly loaded dice one of his guests produced, and paying his losses blithely.

No one could have guessed he was playing a carefully constructed role, and certainly no one could have looked beneath that glittering shell to the fury, bitterness, and grief that had marked its creation.

It was near midnight when Guy Wellman arrived at the boat, bringing with him a man "Duncan" had requested to meet. The party was incredibly noisy by then, the introduction almost shouted, but Keith heard it clearly. Offering his hand to Vincent Arturo, he cordially greeted the man who had destroyed his family.

At four A.M. Keith let himself into the silent hotel suite. Guided only by the faint bedside lamp, he made his way through the sitting room to his bedroom, where he undressed. He took a long, hot shower, washing away the remains of that skin he wore nightly and its taint of smoke and corruption. When he at last felt reasonably clean, he donned a robe and went out into the dark sitting room.

He found a bottle of juice in the suite's wet bar, drinking from it as he sat down in a chair and tried to unwind. His gaze strayed to the closed balcony doors, but he was so tired, so utterly bone weary that he couldn't even swear at himself.

And there was, besides, something else. During this long, tense night, he had realized just how fragile his hold on sanity was. He had politely greeted a man he wanted to strangle with his bare hands, and in that moment he had known how terribly easy it would be to give in to the rage. It wasn't the way he wanted his justice, not with blood on his hands. The urge to release his savage emotions had shaken him badly.

He'd been so close to killing in fury with his own hands that, even now, he wasn't sure what had stopped him. He was even less sure that whatever it had been would stop him next time.

Keith stared at the balcony doors, seeing what he didn't want to see and understanding. He needed an anchor, something to hold him centered when all the wild emotions yanked at him. He hadn't planned for it, hadn't realized it would be necessary. But it was, he saw now. Too much alone in this, too disconnected, he needed a reminder of sanity to keep him from making the all-too-easy step over the edge.

It wouldn't take much to pull him back, he thought. Not much. A sweet voice in the darkness talking of sane things, a soft laugh, the whisper of silk. A distraction, yes, but one this side of madness, to keep him rooted here. He knew it was dangerous, but the greater danger lay in what he might do if he forgot what peace and pleasure felt like.

She probably wouldn't be there, he thought. She'd probably checked out and gone home, back to the man who wanted her to be with him. The gentleness in her voice as much as her words had told Keith she would go a long way to avoid hurting anyone deliberately.

And tonight, he had felt the urge to kill.

He got up and set the empty juice bottle aside, crossing the room to the balcony doors and opening them. He went out into the cool darkness and settled onto the chaise, looking straight ahead without seeing, but listening intently. And as soon as he heard her, he spoke.

"Good morning."

"Good morning," she responded a bit breathlessly. "I thought you must have gone. Yesterday, I mean."

Keith rested his head back against the chaise, feeling his tense muscles begin to unknot. "No, there was . . . something I had to do," *I had to stay away from you. But I can't.*

"You sound tired," she said, the concern in her voice obvious.

"Too tired to sleep. I need to unwind." He wondered, vaguely, if she felt the effect of this as strongly as he did, if she realized how easily they perceived each other's moods—not as strangers, but as friends.

"Do you want to talk?" she asked, a bit hesitant.

Closing his eyes, Keith said, "Your voice is very soothing. If you wouldn't mind—?"

One of her soft laughs escaped her. "I don't mind, but you might. You're so easy to talk to that I probably won't know when to shut up. Just tell me when, and I will."

He smiled slightly. "Agreed."

"What do you want me to talk about?"

"Anything you like." *Anything sane.* "Tell me if you've found any answers for those dawn questions."

"All I'm sure of," she said wryly, "is that I've found more questions. But I did call London, and I told him I wouldn't be coming home."

"For good?" Keith asked, only then aware that he wanted her to say yes.

"Surprisingly enough, that's what I said. He was . . . stunned. He says we have to talk, but I told him I needed time to myself. I don't know how patient he'll be." She paused, then laughed suddenly.

He was intrigued by the sound. "What?"

"Oh, it's absurd! I guess I felt a little self-conscious before, and didn't want to explain. I mean, well, I'm twenty-eight years old; I hardly wanted to say that Daddy had called and ordered me home."

Keith felt a jolt of relief, the depth of which disturbed him. But he managed to say lightly, "Understandable. But there was more, wasn't there? Another reason. You didn't want me to think you might be available?"

"That was part of it," she answered frankly. "So many men seem to think every single woman is looking for involvement. Sometimes it's very annoying. But for some reason, I wanted you to know the truth. It *is* my relationship with my father we've been talking about."

"I see."

"You aren't offended?"

"No, of course not."

"Good," she said with a sigh.

Keith knew an impulse to ask her name or offer his, but ignored it. If he could keep the peculiar relationship between them like this, dawn meetings on a dark balcony, then perhaps he could limit the danger to him—and to her. If he could control at least the depth of this . . .

"In a way," she said reflectively, "you remind me of my father."

"God forbid," Keith said before he could stop himself.

There was a startled silence on the other side of the screen, and then she said, "I meant the tone of your voice sometimes. And your perception."

"Your father is perceptive?" Keith swore

inwardly, telling himself grimly to keep his distance, to remain detached and impersonal.

"About everyone except me. Do you think that's common between fathers and daughters?"

Unbidden, thoughts of his own father and his sister darted through his mind, so painful they might have been knives. "I don't know," he said finally. "My sister . . . always said Dad was her best friend."

"I'm sorry."

Her voice was soft, and so expressive that Keith had to swallow hard before he could speak. "For what?"

"Reminding you of something painful. Sometimes I think people should carry maps with the sore places in their lives marked out in red ink."

"Here there be dragons," Keith said.

"Yes. And then we'd all know to keep out."

Unless you're invited. He didn't say it. He couldn't say it, even though he was finding it impossible to remain impersonal and detached. Her voice pulled at him. He opened his eyes and stared at the graying horizon, resisting; if she pulled him too far back from the edge, he'd never be able to do what he had to do.

If she got too close . . .

"I've decided to take up painting," she said lightly, having obviously judged the worth of his silence and realized she'd been warned off. "I was pretty good at it in school. Maybe it won't come to anything, but I want to try."

"That's the important thing," he murmured. "To try."

The conversation went on in the same vein for a few more minutes, casual but cautious, and by the time the sun rose she had gone back inside. The interlude, as strangely painful as it had become, nonetheless left Keith feeling more grounded, more securely connected to his own reason. Somehow, she was able to do that for him. He didn't know how, but he knew it was something he couldn't afford to give up.

Every morning, they met and talked during the quiet transition of dawn. For the most part, they were relaxed, but at odd moments something else crept between them and caused one or the other to back off warily, to pause and change the subject. Still, the conversations wove a curious web of intimacy between them that deepened day by day.

For nearly a week, Keith found what he needed on the dark balcony. But as the days passed he discovered his thoughts were turning to her more and more often, even at night when all his concentration should have been focused on the role he played. He tried to block the thoughts out, but it grew more difficult with each passing day and night. Even the sure knowledge that she wanted no involvement didn't seem to make a difference. It did no good to tell himself that she seemed satisfied, that she had no desire for a closer relationship. There were no demands in this, no expectations between them; what they had was as transitory as the dawn itself—and yet just as constant.

He might have been able to be content with that, at least for a while longer. She had become his transition between the two lives he was leading, enabling him to keep his balance. He dared not risk losing her. But then one night, the demands of "Duncan's" role went on past dawn, culminating in a subtle game of verbal cat-and-mouse between him and Vincent Arturo that strained Keith to the breaking point.

By the time he returned to his hotel and showered, the sun was well up, and the safety-valve of the quiet morning conversations had been denied to him at a time when it was badly needed. He was days away from seeing an end to it, one way or another, and the tension inside him was so great he felt as if he might explode.

If he had made a different choice, if he'd gone directly to bed instead of stepping out onto his sunny balcony, perhaps everything would have ended differently.

But he did go out to the balcony, knowing she wouldn't be there, wondering if he might see her on the beach. He leaned against the wall and looked down, searching intently. Far up the beach, her red hair shining like a beacon, she was walking along the high-water mark back toward the hotel. It was likely there were other redheads in the hotel, possibly several who ran or walked on the beach in the morning, but he knew her.

Keith went back inside his suite and got dressed. He didn't think about what he was doing until he was crossing the lobby toward the beach, and by then the awareness could only slow his steps— not stop his need for her. He found the path that led to the beach and waited there beneath a curving palm.

Just a look, he told himself reassuringly. To see her face, her eyes. That was all. She'd walk right past him, a stranger, but knowing what she looked like would substitute for their missed conversation this morning.

He wondered, almost idly, if he had finally gone over the edge.

He hadn't expected the instant jolt of familiarity he experienced at the sight of her coming up the path toward him. And he hadn't expected her to stop, no more than a few feet away, her eyes locked with his and holding a shocked expression. He hadn't expected her to be so beautiful.

Beautiful. A pale word to describe her. Her bright hair was a silky mass of loose red curls falling below her shoulders, framing a face so exquisite it stopped his heart. There was no conventional prettiness in those delicate features, nothing of the girl next door, and none of the glamorous "perfection" of a high-fashion model. She possessed the kind of singular beauty that no one, man or woman, would ever question or debate, a rare combination of bone structure, coloring, and features that marked her as a woman who would be lovely all the days of her life.

Keith saw that, acknowledged it vaguely to himself. But it wasn't her overall beauty holding him spellbound, it was her eyes. They were a color he'd never seen before, a pale, almost iridescent green, their depth and clarity so great that they were literally hypnotic.

The sweet voice that had pulled at him combined now with those remarkable eyes. Yes, he understood why her father would consider her an asset. People would talk to her. People would tell her things they wouldn't mention to another soul. The realization went through Keith like a knife.

Abruptly, he turned away.

Erin stood perfectly still, her heart racing. When he turned away, she almost darted forward in protest, but his jerky movement stopped her. He stood with his back to her, his broad shoulders tense, as if he wanted badly to go on but couldn't somehow.

He might have been any age between thirty and forty; his thick, night-black hair was lightly frosted with silver but his lean face was unlined. He was not handsome, but any woman would choose to look at him rather than at beefcake photos in a magazine. Once seen, his face would never be forgotten. His features were strong, from his high cheekbones and aquiline nose to the stubborn jaw and slightly cleft chin. Violet eyes were hooded by heavy lids, enigmatic but curiously brilliant, and set beneath flying brows that lent his hard face a saturnine air at odds with the generous curve of his mouth.

She knew who he was, even though everything about him was unexpected. Erin was a tall woman, but he towered over her. She guessed he was at least three inches over six feet. And he had the imposing build to match his height. The jeans and casual knit shirt he wore did nothing to disguise commanding shoulders, a massive chest, hard, narrow waist and hips, and powerful thighs. His vitality and force were obvious, as was the fact that heredity and an active life had given him a natural strength few men could command no matter how many hours they worked out in gyms.

Time had seemed to stop. It could have been hours or seconds only, a minute perhaps before he turned slowly back around to face her.

If, at that moment, Erin had been asked to define the word dangerous, she would have pointed unhesitatingly at him. Not because he was so obviously powerful physically, but because she could *feel* the danger in him, like an aura that was almost visible. She had felt that only once before in her life, while gazing in fascination at an adult male lion through the bars of his cage; a beautiful creature, seemingly so lazy and unthreatening, but holding in his eyes the look of an unpredictable beast that could be caged but never tamed.

This lion wasn't caged, but despite her awareness of danger Erin felt no fear of him. And she wondered if he felt it, too, this strange bond between them, a thing of instinct and emotion rather than knowledge or understanding.

"Good morning," he said, his deep voice the way it had been that first morning, a bit guarded. "I'm Keith Donovan."

There was no need at all to add explanations, she thought. Names and faces might be strange, but they knew each other. "Erin Prentice," she said, her own voice a little husky.

He half nodded. "Will you have breakfast with me, Erin Prentice?"

Fearless of him or not, she should have at least hesitated, but it never crossed her mind to do so. "Yes, I will."

He smiled, the curve of his mouth softening his hard face into one that was surprisingly charming. "I hoped you would. The terrace restaurant here serves the best food. Shall we?" He didn't offer to take her hand or arm, but merely gestured slightly.

Suddenly conscious of her windblown hair, baggy sweatpants, and overlarge T-shirt, Erin said, "I should change—"

"You must know you're beautiful," he said.

She felt a faint shock, not because of what he said but of how he said it. He sounded matter of fact, if not indifferent. Taking little notice of her own appearance when she was alone, Erin had nonetheless been taught all her life to show her best face to the world, and since it had been drummed into her that her face and smile were her best—if not only—assets, this man's dispassionate acknowledgment of her looks was as rare as it was welcome.

She closed the distance between them slowly, at a loss to know how she could respond to his statement. He didn't appear to expect a response, however, and they walked across the lobby to the terrace restaurant in silence.

It wasn't until they were seated on the terrace, once more in the sunshine, that he spoke again. "Did I offend you? I didn't mean to."

Erin shook her head a bit helplessly. "How could you have offended me?"

His smile dawned again. "I might have been implying that you were vain and *had* to know how beautiful you are. I wasn't, though. It's just that I imagine you've been hearing compliments on your looks all your life."

She was granted a few moments to pull herself together after that curiously impassive statement, since the waiter came to pour coffee and take their orders. Grateful that he wasn't the kind of man who automatically ordered food for his companion, she gave the waiter her order and then watched Keith as he did the same.

When they were alone again, she said lightly, "It's only a matter of good genes."

"Yes, I know."

Erin felt a spurt of annoyance, and had to laugh at herself. To his questioning look, she said wryly, "I've always hated being taken at face value—but I seem to have gotten used to it."

"Feeling insulted because I agreed you had nothing to do with how you look?"

"Yes. Absurd, isn't it?"

His strangely vivid gaze rested on her face, but was still shuttered and impossible for her to read.

"No, not if you've been taught to believe how you look is the biggest part of who you are."

It occurred to Erin then that Keith Donovan would never tell her what he thought she wanted to hear. He would not make pretty speeches, pay charming compliments, or say anything he didn't honestly mean. She was accustomed to dealing with all kinds of people, but in the social and diplomatic circles in which she'd come of age, Keith's brand of candor was something she had never encountered.

She felt herself smiling. "I think that's been one of my problems. It doesn't seem to be one of yours. Are you impervious to attractive women, Keith?" She thought she saw something in his eyes flare when she said his name, but there was no other change of expression on his faintly smiling face.

"To call you attractive," he said in that dispassionate tone, which robbed his words of compliment, "is like calling the ocean wet; the word doesn't begin to describe the subject. Am I impervious to beauty? No. Even a marble statue would turn his head when you walked by. Would I have asked you to breakfast if you'd been ordinarily pretty or even plain—probably. I wanted to meet you. Believe that or not, it's up to you."

"You were attracted by my mind?" she murmured.

"Your voice," he replied calmly. "I don't know enough of your mind. Yet."

Erin looked at him wonderingly. "Ninety-nine men out of a hundred in my experience would have swallowed that bait without even bothering to chew on it."

Real amusement gleamed in his eyes. "I don't doubt that's just what you have experienced."

"What makes you different?"

He seemed to hesitate, then spoke slowly, the amusement gone, his eyes dimmed. "My sister was beautiful, like you. Different coloring, but . . . heads turned when she walked by. People stared at her in absolute astonishment. I know what she went through. I know what you've gone through, Erin."

Erin could see the sign warning her of dragons, but the pain she sensed made her ask, "Is your sister—?"

"Killed. In a car . . . accident. Over a year ago."

"I'm sorry. I'm so sorry, Keith."

A quick smile, the automatic acknowledgment of sympathy, was his only response as he leaned back to allow the waiter to serve him. Erin wondered if he would say anything more about his sister, but when the waiter had gone he reverted to the discussion about beauty.

"Most people firmly believe that extreme beauty is a blessing, that it opens doors without effort. It isn't true, of course, but even that isn't the worst of it. We've all been conditioned to judge by appearance. We wrap presents in shiny paper and package cereals in colorful boxes, and stick nice, neat labels on everything we possibly can. Your label reads 'beautiful.' So ninety-nine men out of a hundred will never see past that label even while they assure you it's your mind they were attracted to in the first place."

"And the hundredth man?" Erin asked softly.

Keith dropped his gaze to his plate for an instant, and when he looked at her again there was something almost grim in his expression. "The hundredth man heard a sweet voice on a dark balcony," he said, his own voice one she'd never heard from him before.

Erin wasn't a blushing woman, she'd been flattered by too many men and stared at by too many
strangers to be easily disturbed or embarrassed.
But she felt heat rise in her face now, and it was
strangely difficult to catch her breath. The sudden change from dispassionate to grindingly intense emotion had thrown her off balance, but it
was more than that, and even though she knew
it she couldn't define what it was.

One somewhat grim statement, delivered in a
voice that had been harsh around the edges, and
she felt . . . What did she feel? Confused, she bent
her head over her own plate and began eating her
breakfast, though she had no idea at all of what
it was she was eating.

What is this? The question was loud in her
mind, bewildered and not quite, but almost afraid.
In the first moments of meeting him, her mind
had been so active she hadn't allowed herself to
realize that a mental response wasn't the only
thing she felt toward him. But now she could feel
that deeper, more primitive response in every
throbbing nerve of her body, and she was at a
loss to account for it.

She had never admired very big men, feeling
overpowered by them; she had preferred fair men
to dark as far back as she could recall; and this
man's hawklike face, though certainly compelling, was not handsome and was even—without
the surprisingly charming smile—rather harsh.
In addition to all that, she was still in the process
of adjusting her responses to a man who said he
was—and certainly appeared to be—indifferent to
the way she looked. As welcome as that might
be, it was something she had never encountered
before and had found a bit unnerving.

And he hadn't *said* anything to do this to her.

Had he? If any other man had said that about a sweet voice on a dark balcony, she thought she would have laughed. But when he said it, she felt as if some barrier inside herself had melted instantly in the face of an explosion of heat. What was wrong with her?

"I didn't plan on this," Keith said roughly, almost angrily. "I thought it would be enough, just to talk to you. But it isn't, Erin. It isn't enough. What have you done to me?"

"I—I didn't do anything."

"Yes, you did. You haunted me until I couldn't think of anything else, until—" He broke off abruptly.

She waited, head bent, conscious of the most amazing sensations inside herself. She felt hot and cold, tense yet strangely weak, her heart thudding wildly. The desire in his stormy voice was as clear as if it were etched in stone or blazing in neon, and she wondered dazedly how he could be making love to her without either touching her or uttering a single caressing word.

The strange, angry urgency in his voice made her think of some half-savage creature who knew he needed and yet struggled fiercely not to give in.

"Erin?"

She looked up shyly, meeting his steady gaze.

"I'm sorry." His voice was even, the harsh edges smoothed away, and his face was completely expressionless. "I had no right to push."

"Was that what you did?"

"We both know it. You've made it plain you aren't looking for involvement. I have to respect your decision."

Erin realized she should accept what he said. She should nod and change the subject so that this breakfast would be, like the dawn discussions, just an undemanding interlude. But somehow, without her volition, she heard herself ask, "Are you looking for involvement?"

"I wasn't." He hesitated, then added in a hard tone, "I shouldn't have come down this morning. It would have been better if things had gone on the way they were."

She felt an odd pang, but kept her voice quiet. "Why would it have been better? Nameless . . . faceless . . ."

"You can't deny you wanted it that way."

"No, I can't. At first, that was what I wanted. But not now. Not for days." Her voice became a little unsteady as his expression became remote. "I'm sorry if you don't like hearing that, but it's the truth."

"Erin—"

She managed a wry laugh, dropping her gaze to her half-empty plate. "Well, that ought to teach me a lesson. I should thank you, and I do. For the first time in my life, what I look like doesn't seem to matter—and there's obviously nothing else about me *to* matter. A very valuable lesson."

"Erin, stop it." He reached across the table suddenly, his powerful hand covering her slim one and grasping it strongly. "It has nothing to do with you."

"Doesn't it?" She looked up at him, a tiny frown between her brows. "I don't know what's wrong with me."

Keith knew, and he knew it was his fault. Her beauty had been her shield, and since no one had apparently tried to get past that barrier, her emotions had remained largely untouched. Whether courted or rejected, she had been able to tell herself it was because of *that*, because of the way she looked. Then he had said her beauty was a fortunate combination of genes and nothing more, and with the shield gone his seeming rejection had touched her rawest vulnerability.

He hadn't meant to blow hot and then cold, to make his desire so obvious to her that she had, surprisingly and shyly, responded before he could withdraw without hurting her. He had hurt her, and he knew it. What he didn't know was where it would end if he didn't back off right now.

"There's nothing wrong with you," he told her, his voice steady.

She was still frowning. "There must be. I feel so strange." Abruptly, she pulled her hand free and leaned back, her face settling into a polite mask. "I'm sorry. I must have forgotten how to flirt. I was taking it all too seriously, wasn't I? Never mind. It's funny, though; I've danced with princes and never lost my head when even Dad thought I might."

"Erin, the timing's lousy, that's all. It has nothing to do with you."

She smiled. "Stop frowning, Keith. I obviously misunderstood, and there's no harm done. Shouldn't you be getting some rest?"

Keith signaled the waiter and signed the check, but when they rose he took her hand firmly in his. She didn't protest or say anything at all until he led her through the lobby and back toward the beach.

"Where are we going?"

"We have to talk."

An uncertain laugh escaped her. "The men in my life always want to talk."

He led her partway down the path, then angled off away from the cabanas and the increasing activity on the beach. In this area, the hotel provided a small gardenlike area with a neat lawn, well-tended palms and shrubs, and cosy little benches scattered invitingly in the shade. No one else was taking advantage of the invitation—not that Keith would have given a damn.

Stopping near one of the benches, he turned to face her, releasing her hand because he didn't trust himself to go on touching her. It had hit him with brutal force as he looked at her across the table, a wave of desire so powerful that he had only barely been able to control it. Until then, he had been fine, he thought, completely able to think of the shared breakfast as just another interlude. Her eyes and voice had tugged at him, but he had managed to hold himself steady.

He was a long way from steady now, and he knew it.

"Keith, there's no need to talk about this," Erin said in a firm voice. "It isn't important—"

"The hell it isn't. You *did* misunderstand, and I don't know how to convince you without making bad worse." He hesitated, then said flatly, "Dammit, Erin, I want you. Do you understand that? I want you."

She stared up at him, faint color blooming and then fading in her cheeks, confused and beginning to be angry about it. "No, I don't understand! Is this pity? Are you trying to be kind to a stupid woman who threw herself at you?" It occurred to her, vaguely, that she and Keith were still reacting to each other as if they weren't strangers, but her own emotions were so chaotic that she hardly paid attention to the uniqueness of the entire situation.

"You didn't throw yourself at me." He was trying very hard to keep his voice calm. "I'm the one who crossed the line, and I *shouldn't* have. Erin, you don't know me, but I sure as hell do. I'm no prize even in a good mood, and I'm a bad-tempered bastard most of the time. I'd hurt you without meaning to, and I'm not going to let that happen."

"Oh, excuse me, I didn't realize you were being noble," Erin snapped, too angry to wonder where it was all coming from.

He gritted his teeth visibly, his striking eyes more brilliant than ever under heavy lids. "Nobility might fit those princes you danced with, but don't throw it at me."

"It certainly doesn't fit you," she shot back at him. "So why don't you stop trying to be something you aren't?"

"All I'm *trying* to do is keep you from making the worst mistake of your life! What do you want, Erin, a fling? You want to go up to one of our rooms and climb into bed with a man whose name you didn't know until an hour ago? Is that the way you mean to prove to your father that you aren't his little girl any more?"

She slapped him.

In the utter silence that followed, they stared at each other, both pale, the reddened imprint of her fingers marking his cheek. Her eyes were wide, almost blind, her breasts rising and falling rapidly beneath the thin cotton of her T-shirt. His face was stony, his mouth a grim slash.

Then an odd little sound escaped Erin, not nearly a laugh, and she said unsteadily, "It must be that, mustn't it? The reason. Because it doesn't make any sense. You are a stranger. And I can't feel like this about a stranger without some reason. So it must be that. It must be—"

Keith closed his eyes briefly, then reached out and pulled her roughly into his arms. "I'm sorry," he muttered in a rasping voice, holding her strongly against him.

She was stiff, but not struggling, her hands lying still on his chest. "No, if I hadn't been so stupid, you wouldn't have said it—And it was the truth, I shouldn't have hit you for telling the truth—"

"Shhhh." He turned her face up, one big hand surrounding it with surprising gentleness. "It wasn't the truth. Look at me, Erin."

Tumbling from one emotion to another since she had first seen him, Erin was by then almost numb. The arm holding her so close to him was hard but not painful, the hand on her face gentle, and his deep voice softer than she'd ever heard it. She wanted to cry, but obediently raised her eyes to meet his.

"It wasn't the truth," he repeated quietly. "If you don't know you could never be so reckless, well at least I do."

"Then why did you say it?" she whispered.

A nerve throbbed at one corner of his mouth. "Maybe I wanted it to be true. Maybe I hoped it would shock you enough that you'd realize how insane this is and tell me to go to hell."

She conjured a rueful smile. "I don't seem to have enough pride to tell you to go anywhere at all."

Three

The arm around her tightened, and his hand
slipped down to enclose her throat. Fleetingly,
Erin thought that he could break her neck quite
easily. She might have been forgiven for wondering if he meant to because his face looked as
stony as it had when she'd slapped him, almost
cruel in its fixed expression of grim anger. But
Erin didn't wonder. She met his glittering eyes
with no fear in her own, and she reached out to
touch his lean cheek.

"Don't be angry," she murmured. "I can't help
it." For the first time in her life, she felt totally
comfortable in revealing her own emotions, and
if there was surprise in that, she didn't think
about it, because everything seemed so natural
with him. Talking to him, fighting with him,
touching him—it all felt incredibly familiar. Her
deepest instincts told her their tranquil dawn
interludes had woven a link between her and this
man, and a certainty beyond reason insisted the
connection was terribly important to them both.

For an instant after her soft words, his face

remained unyielding, but then something changed. It wasn't a lessening of intensity, but a shifting. Anger was replaced by another emotion that gleamed in his eyes.

"Dammit, Erin," he said roughly, his hand slipping to the nape of her neck, beneath her thick hair. He lowered his head and covered her parted lips with his own.

He had stated with utter certainty that she wasn't reckless enough to sleep with a stranger in order to prove a point to her father, but Erin knew she was reckless enough to follow blindly wherever this might lead. Or maybe it wasn't recklessness. Maybe it was conviction. All she knew for sure was that she had to be in his arms. She *had* to.

It wasn't a first kiss, a seeking, tentative thing; he kissed her with stark desire, the force in him that was vital and compelling, sweeping over her in a tidal wave of demand. She had believed she wanted no demands, no expectations, but everything in her rose explosively now to meet his passion.

Her arms slid around his lean waist as she pressed herself even closer, something in her delighting in the sensation of being small and enclosed in his powerful embrace. His body was so hard, and hers fit so well against him. Heat spread through her in pulsing bursts and all her senses seemed to come rawly alive as though nothing had ever touched them before.

If she had been granted a moment to think then, Erin might well have run from this, from him. She was, ordinarily, a woman of mild feelings, unaccustomed to violent highs and lows; if it had been otherwise, she could never have accepted her father's control over her life for so long. She had never understood turbulent emotions because she had never felt them, had never believed herself capable of such wildness, and the very thought of losing control emotionally was frightening to her.

But she was given no time to feel wariness or fear, no chance to turn away from this and run. The force of him overwhelmed everything except the instant, searing strength of her own response.

With her senses so vibrantly alive, she heard a faint little sound and felt it in her throat, a purr of pleasure that was alien and dimly shocking because she had never before made a sound like that. Her fingers were exploring the hard muscles of his back, and her breasts throbbed almost painfully against his massive chest as if all the veins had expanded and filled with hot blood. The thrust of his tongue was a small possession she welcomed eagerly, and her body moved unconsciously, seeking and inviting a much greater intimacy.

Keith hadn't meant for this to happen. With what little coherent thought left to him, he told himself that his own lack of control was due to his tension, the pressure he was under, and the long months of obsessive planning that had left no room for a personal life of any kind. He was a sensual man by nature, not accustomed to denying himself, and *that* was why . . . It was just physical desire, only lust.

Nothing else made sense.

But the same thread of reason to which he grimly clung insisted there was more to it than simple lust. Much more, even though he couldn't put a name to it. What his body demanded wasn't mere release—it was joining. He wanted, needed, to become a part of her, to merge the two of them together until there was no separateness, until they were bound immutably together. And he thought she wanted the same thing. She was so alive in his arms, so utterly responsive, and he wanted her with a reckless, heedless need almost impossible to fight.

Almost. But the thread of sanity held in his mind, and it was enough—barely—to give him the will to end that scorching kiss and set her away from him. He kept his hands on her hips, holding her away, trying to control his ragged breathing enough to say something, anything, that would stop them before it was too late . . . before he pulled them both over the edge.

She was staring at him, her eyes wide and dazed, her parted lips a little swollen from the fierce pressure of his. Pushed back away from him, she had grasped handfuls of his shirt as if unconsciously determined not to let go of him.

"No," he said finally, his voice little more than a hoarse rasp.

"Why?" she whispered, not even vaguely surprised that she was, quite definitely, throwing herself at him now. It didn't make any sense, none of it did, but she was caught up in something that was rushing forward and she couldn't stop it, couldn't stop herself. She couldn't even stop the naked words, "I want you too. You know that. You have to know it."

Keith managed to get his breathing under control, but his willpower was still hanging by a mere thread and she wasn't helping any. "Erin, you don't know what you want. You've cut one tie to a domineering man, don't be so quick to form another."

"Is that what you are? A domineering man?" She wondered why he was doing this, because that didn't make sense either. He wanted her, but was obviously determined that they wouldn't be lovers, and she didn't understand why.

"Bet on it."

"I don't think so." She shook her head as if it didn't really matter, but her beautiful face expressed puzzlement and hurt, a dawning realization. "You just don't want—complications. Is that it? You're afraid I'd cling." She seemed to notice her deathgrip on his shirt for the first time, and slowly released the material. "Maybe you're right. I don't seem to have any pride at all."

"Erin—"

In a very steady voice, she said, "Tell me you've got a wife and kids back in Topeka. Or that you're a convicted ax murderer or gunrunner or something. Tell me something, Keith. Tell me why."

He forced his hands to let go of her. In the most even voice he could manage, he said, "Erin, this is happening too fast, you know that. You aren't thinking clearly."

"But you are?"

"I have to. I don't want to hurt you, and I think that's what would happen. I wouldn't be good for you. I wouldn't be good for anyone right now."

"Would I be good for you?"

"I don't know."

"Is there a wife? Kids?"

Keith shook his head, angry at himself because he was unable to tell her the one thing that would probably make her run from him in horror. The truth. *I came here to destroy two men.* He couldn't tell her that. He couldn't stand here and see her face change if he told her that.

Erin crossed her arms beneath her breasts, almost hugging herself as she stared up at him. The rosy flush of desire had faded, leaving her pale. "You wouldn't be good for me. Why can't I simply accept what you say?" She chuckled, the uncertain sound of someone stranded in a boat that had lost its rudder.

He instinctively lifted a hand toward her, but she stepped back quickly.

"Damn you, don't be kind." Her voice was low and rapid. "I feel enough of a fool without that. I—I'm sorry. Sorry about the whole thing. Good-bye, Keith."

He took two steps after her before he could stop himself, then stood gazing across the little garden at nothing. He felt like the worst kind of bastard because of what he'd done to her. And to himself. No matter how many times he told himself it was better this way, that he would surely have hurt her even if the danger of the situation around him had never touched her, the emotional certainty he should have felt was absent.

It was against his very nature to avoid facing anything, no matter how disturbing or painful, and in pushing her away so forcefully he was trying to evade something that promised to be both. But what choice did he have? Even assuming that Erin could be content not knowing where he disappeared to every evening, that she wouldn't eventually expect the truth from him, what right did he have to become her lover when a single misstep could mean his death? It was his risk, not hers, and he couldn't make her a part of his life when any future at all was so uncertain, when even the present was dangerous and unpredictable.

Even setting that aside, the violent emotions trapped inside him—the grief and fury and bitterness—made his temper brittle, and the role he had to play left him so edgy he could hardly live with himself. All his emotional energy was bound up in maintaining his balance in that other life he was leading; there was very little left for a normal life. What would that do to her? How could he be a lover when so many of the emotions driving him were negative ones?

She was vulnerable, he knew. Hers was a gentle heart, and he'd never forgive himself if he did anything to damage her. He had felt her surprise at the intensity of her own response to him, and it told him more than she probably realized. For whatever inexplicable reason—and he didn't pretend to understand either her feelings or his own—his reckless desire triggered hers in a way she'd never felt before, and the sheer power of her desire had overwhelmed her.

He knew that was true, because it had happened to him too. The difference between them was that he knew all the odds against them—and she didn't.

After a while, realizing his weariness was making thoughts chase each other around in his head uselessly, Keith went back into the hotel and up to his room. He wasn't planning on going out tonight, but knew it was smarter to sleep when he could just in case.

Needing to sleep, however, was one thing; being able to was something else. It was past noon before he finally slipped into a restless, uneasy sleep, and when he woke around six he wondered if it had been worth the effort. A shower chased away most of the cobwebs and coffee scattered the rest, but he found it no easier to think now than he had that morning.

Even though common sense told him to, he knew for certain he couldn't leave things the way they were between him and Erin. Leaving it alone, just letting it end so abruptly, was impossible for him. He couldn't stand the thought of knowing he had hurt her. Yet she was too firmly in his head, distracting him until he could hardly think of anything but her; she had gotten too close.

Unfortunately for both of them, pushing her away physically had done nothing to change the situation. In fact, it was worse now, because there was a beautiful face and haunting eyes to go with the sweet voice, and all of her was so damned unforgettable.

He didn't go to the connecting doors, but out into the hallway to her door. He thought as he knocked quietly that she had every reason to tell him to go to hell, and no reason at all to want to see him again. But the door opened.

"May I talk to you?" he asked. She was wearing some kind of lounging outfit, pants and a loose, peasant-type top made of terrycloth, the same pale green as her eyes. With her creamy skin and bright hair she was a heartbreakingly gorgeous sight. For the first time, he wondered if her absence from his side was why there had been a constant ache in his chest since this morning. Quickly, he pushed the thought aside.

Erin hesitated, then stepped back to allow him to enter. He went into the sitting room, absently noticing a large sketchpad on the table near the balcony doors and remembering that she had decided to take up artwork. There was a charcoal drawing on the top page, but he didn't go near enough to see what it was. He turned to face Erin, and she spoke before he could.

"You didn't have to come here, you know." Her voice was soft, her face expressionless. "I've already decided to leave, so—"

"Don't," he said involuntarily.

She shook her head. "What was it you said about me, that I didn't know what I wanted? That seems to be your problem."

"I know what I want. I also know what I can't have."

Erin's chin lifted slightly and a spark of anger showed in her eyes. "Do you mind? I really don't want to hear that kind of statement again. I don't know what game you're playing, Keith, but you can count me out. I may have thrown my pride to the winds with you this morning, but I've stopped that now. I'm not a masochist."

Keith shoved his hands into his pockets, fighting the insane urge to reach out and yank her into his arms. "I'm sorry, Erin. I never meant to hurt you. And it wasn't—isn't—a game. You have to understand."

She didn't understand, and hours of grappling with her own emotions had left Erin in a precarious balance on the edge of control. She was baffled by him, by the contrast between his words and his actions. He kept saying no and yet he couldn't seem to stay away, couldn't close the door between them. She had the consolation of knowing that this was difficult for him, but it didn't help at all because she didn't understand why he was fighting so hard.

And complicating the whole thing was her confused certainty that he really was concerned about *her*, that he was convinced he would hurt her, and was determined not to. His sensitivity argued against his own words. If he cared so much about not hurting her, then how could he be capable of doing it? Erin had held her own with men who had made careers of being enigmatic, but Keith had her totally bewildered.

During the last hours, she had told herself he'd

been right this morning; she didn't know what she wanted. He was the first man she had felt so—so overwhelmed by, and thinking clearly about him seemed beyond her. All her instincts told her there was a great deal of anger in him, that he was a dangerous man, and yet she didn't feel the least threat from or fear of him. What she felt, more than anything else, was a sense of certainty, of conviction.

She sighed. What good was her confidence when he struggled so hard against it? No good.

Erin squared her shoulders and met his intense gaze with all the coolness she could muster. "If you've said what you came here for, then please leave. I have to finish packing."

"I don't want you to go," he said.

She wasn't given to emotional gestures, but if there had been something heavy nearby, Erin would have thrown it at him. Instead, she crossed her arms beneath her breasts and counted silently to ten. Then, carefully, she said, "*I* want to go."

"Do you?"

"Stop it, Keith!" She looked around a little wildly, but there was nothing heavy close by.

An odd laugh escaped him. "I know—I'm not being consistent."

"Consistent? You're driving me crazy!" She controlled herself with an effort. "I don't want to do this. Do you understand? I don't want to feel like this. Maybe you enjoy stormy, bewildering relationships, but I don't." Even as her normally soft and gentle voice rose on the last words, Erin was completely unconscious of the transformation taking place inside her; she couldn't know that by tapping into the depths of her emotions, Keith had opened a door she hadn't realized was there.

Born into an elegant and ordered life, Erin had

been insulated by her environment as much as by her looks. Molded first by the private schools whose job it was to turn out gracious and accomplished ladies, and then by the coolly dominant father who favored tranquil voices and graceful manners. Erin had never even suspected there was fire in her nature. She had never cared enough about anything or anyone to fight.

But here was Keith. He was so strong that his drive was like a visible aura, so complex that he confused her totally. Far from talking to her almost unconsciously and unguardedly as so many men did, he was blunt, abrupt, intense, and enigmatic. There was anger in him, and danger, and nothing in Erin's experience had taught her how to cope with such an explosive combination.

All she had left was instinct.

If there had been no fire in her own nature, being engulfed in his force could have burned her badly, leaving her, by this point, totally shattered and wanting only a dark corner in which to hide and lick her wounds. If she had been the completely gentle woman they both believed her to be, she could never have held her own with him. But by running hot and cold, Keith had blown on smoldering embers neither of them had recognized, and that fire was burning now.

"I *will not* play games with you," she said, almost spitting in her anger. "And I'm not about to stick around here while you make up your mind whether you have the inclination to get involved with me."

"I think you know what my inclination is," he murmured, eyes narrowed as he gazed at her.

Her eyes flashed at him. "There you go again! Saying yes in one breath and no in the next. Well, forget it, Keith. I value myself slightly above a doormat. I might have acted like one earlier today, but don't expect a repeat performance."

"You didn't act like a doormat," he said. "You acted like a very passionate woman. I should have paid closer attention."

Erin took three rapid steps away from him and then returned to glare at him. In a conversational tone, she said, "Why am I not calling the manager and having you hauled out of here?"

"Because you're three parts spitfire," Keith said, still gazing at her in fascination.

She made a sound that might have been mistaken for a snarl, and said between gritted teeth, "Go away. Leave."

Even more than before, Keith was torn. This new side of her, promising definite fireworks, was mesmerizing, and something his own vigorous nature was strongly attracted toward. If he had felt drawn to her before, it was nothing compared to the pull he felt now. Only the magnetism of her had changed—but none of the rest seemed so important now, while he was with her.

"Did you hear me?" she demanded.

"Loud and clear."

"Then why are you still here?"

He almost smiled at that aggrieved question. "Erin, would you like to have dinner with me?"

"No," she snapped.

"Would you like to go to bed with me?"

Her mouth opened and then closed, and she stared at him for at least half a minute before saying, "You are the most maddening man I have ever met in my life."

"Then you're forewarned." This time, he did smile. "I'm afraid I won't be good for you, but I can't seem to be reasonable about this. I have tried . . . You look surprised," he added, trying not to laugh.

"Then my face is kinder than my thoughts," she said in a wondering tone of voice. "I feel amazed. Staggered. Stunned. You actually believe I'd go to bed with you after all this?"

"I'm lower than scum for suggesting it, I know," he said.

Erin turned away abruptly and went to the open balcony doors. Her back was stiff, and she didn't turn around to face him. "I think I hate you," she said coldly.

"I wouldn't be at all surprised."

"Arrogant bastard."

"Undoubtedly."

"Any woman crazy enough to get involved with you deserves everything she gets."

"Uh-huh. Eight o'clock okay with you for dinner?"

"Aren't you working?"

"Not tonight."

"Oh."

"Is eight o'clock all right?" he repeated.

"Yes."

"I'll come back for you in an hour," Keith said matter of factly, and left before she could change her mind.

It was a good minute before Erin turned to stare at the empty room. "I'm out of my mind," she said in a judicious tone. "I am certifiably mad." Moving carefully, she sat down at the small table and stared at her opened sketchpad.

The sketch, done in a fury of confused emotion during the afternoon, was of Keith. Without conceit, Erin knew it was good. The stark black-and-white portrait showed a complex man whose compelling face was brooding and sensual. There were secrets in the hooded eyes and a devilish tilt to the eyebrows, and his mouth was curved in a dangerous smile.

"I should have drawn horns on you," she muttered, and firmly closed the sketchpad.

Erin had never felt so many diverse emotions all jumbled together inside her. Passion, hurt, fury, indignation, and a wholly unwilling and somewhat staggered amusement at the sheer nerve of the man. Since the morning, she'd ridden an emotional tidal wave, and had no idea where it was taking her.

It was unnerving to discover she was unwilling to save herself, and she was actually looking forward to the rest of the ride.

She thought about that while she was getting ready, unable to reach any conclusion except that she was obviously demented. The man was a devil, evidently amusing himself by yanking her around on the end of an emotional string, and she ought to have her head examined for letting him get away with it. On second thought, she didn't need her head examined; she *knew* she was crazy.

She was also crazy for choosing to wear a gold dress that shimmered faintly with every move she made. It was vaguely Grecian in design, leaving one shoulder bare and clinging closely to her body from breasts to hips before falling more loosely in a knee-length skirt. She knew the color suited her, and the style emphasized every curve. Delicate sandals showed off trim ankles and slender legs, and her loose hairstyle implied less control and dignity than was at all wise.

Dressed for battle, she thought somewhat grimly, and didn't like to consider what that might mean.

The flowers that arrived at a quarter to eight

didn't do much to clarify her mood—they just disconcerted her even more. He'd sent roses. White roses. She hoped the choice had been automatic or that of the hotel florist; as well as she remembered, white roses symbolized eternity. No message on the card, just his name, bold enough to belong to any villain.

By the time she went to answer the knock on her door at eight, Erin was in a tenuous state best described as guarded. The man was a warlock, and she was bewitched—there was no other explanation for it.

When she opened the door, Keith took one look at the dress she had chosen to wear and said simply, "Gold is your color."

"Thank you. And thank you for the flowers."

His crooked smile dawned. "I would have brought them myself, but I figured you'd throw them in my face."

"Perceptive of you."

"She's still feeling hostile," he murmured, stepping back so she could come out into the hall.

"Do admit she has reason," Erin retorted, pulling her door shut behind her.

"I'll admit it." He took her arm in a light grasp as they walked toward the elevator. "I'll even admit that I'll probably get worse before I get better."

Vaguely wishing he didn't look so devastating in a formal suit and tie, Erin said in a very polite tone, "Oh, are you planning to get better?".

He chuckled. "I'm hoping you can reform me."

Erin glanced up at him, very conscious of the intensity lurking beneath his composed surface. She was wary of this new mood of his, and painfully aware of how quickly and easily she'd caved in when he asked her to dinner. She hadn't even been able to *pretend* she had any pride left. Bewitched, that was it. The man had her bewitched and beguiled, and she wasn't even sure how he'd managed to do it. She didn't respond to his comment, remaining silent as they took the elevator down and walked across the lobby to the most elegant restaurant the hotel boasted.

She could feel the stares as they were conducted to their table, and while that was a familiar sensation, what she sensed in Keith was not. He was, she realized in surprise, focused on *her* totally. He was completely indifferent to the eyes on them, and there was nothing proprietary or arrogantly possessive in the way he held her arm. Having been regarded by many men as an ornament they displayed proudly in public, Erin had grown to hate entering any crowded room on a man's arm; they always seemed to feel that there was some kind of male triumph in being the escort of a woman other men watched.

She was accustomed to most men acting differently when they were with her in public. The most quiet and unassuming man tended to become more assertive, to sit taller and speak louder, while the ones with natural confidence surrounded her with an air of intimacy as though they were lovers.

But not Keith. He was exactly the same in public as in private, and as maddening as she found him she was very grateful for that evidence of consistency.

"You're smiling," he noted as the waiter left with their drink orders.

She looked him in the eye, and said calmly, "You have your secrets—I have mine."

"Which is as it should be," he said.

Erin decided not to pursue the subject.

"Have you canceled your plans to leave?" he asked, as if he hadn't expected her to reply to the statement.

"Not exactly."

"What does that mean—exactly?"

She sighed. "It means that I have airline reservations for tomorrow afternoon."

He gazed steadily at her, his expression unreadable. "I see. So tonight will determine whether you'll get on the plane."

It didn't sound like a question, but Erin knew it was. She managed a shrug, and hoped she didn't look defensive.

Keith didn't say anything until their waiter had delivered the drinks and left, and when he did speak his voice was very quiet. "I know you're angry, and I can't blame you. I can't even explain why I've been so . . . contradictory."

"Try," she requested evenly.

He shook his head a little, more, it seemed, at himself than at her. "Erin, my life is very complicated right now. I'm under a lot of pressure, and it's having a negative effect on me. On my emotions, my temper."

"Pressure? From what?" As curious about the careful way he was telling her this as she was about what he was saying, Erin listened intently as she tried to pick up subtle nuances in his deep voice.

"From my work. Work I don't want to talk about. I know it isn't fair to you, and I'm sorry, but that's the way it has to be. I'm not a criminal. I'm not doing anything illegal. In another week, two at most, my work here will be finished."

"And then?"

That, Keith thought, was a loaded question. To see the end of what had obsessed him for nearly a year . . . what would it do to him? How would it change him? Could he ever go back to being the man he had been before all this began? He didn't know. And all he could do was to answer Erin's question in the simplest way possible.

"Then the pressure will be gone. I have a home in New York, a business. A normal life."

Erin gazed at him, trying to understand. "What you're doing here isn't a part of your normal life?"

"No, this is something else. Something I have to do."

"A man of mystery," she murmured.

"Hardly. The point is, I won't be a very good . . . companion until my work's finished. I know that I should escort you to the plane tomorrow, let you go. Later, when I'm through here, I could follow you."

"But?" Erin prompted when he fell silent and looked at her broodingly.

"But . . . no matter how many times I tell myself to do that, I can't seem to listen to reason. This is the worst possible time to begin any kind of relationship, but I don't want you to go. I'm selfish, Erin. I want you with me. On my terms."

The waiter came to take their orders then, allowing Erin a few moments to gather her thoughts. She ordered automatically, hardly paying attention to her choices, her mind in turmoil.

His terms? She thought she knew what those would be. No commitment, no demands—and no questions. Any woman would be a fool to accept that, she knew. Where he went and what he did at night would be none of her business, that half of his life closed to her. Even if it were only a week or two, she had heard the strain and edginess in his voice during their dawn conversations, had sensed the smoldering anger in him, and even though she wasn't afraid of him, how could she cope with emotions like that when she had no understanding of the source?

He wasn't a criminal, he'd said, and what he was doing was not illegal. But he wouldn't talk about it, except to say the pressure was having a negative effect on him. It wasn't a part of his "normal" life, it was something he had to do. Alone. Something that was, she was very much afraid, tearing him up inside. And he wouldn't share that with her, wouldn't explain what was going on.

And what was he asking of her, really? Did he want no more than a brief affair, an outlet for the physical tensions left by these unnamed pressures? Did he want her only because of the explosive passion they'd both felt? Had it really been her voice on a dark balcony that had drawn him, or had he merely needed a woman and sensed her vulnerability?

The questions were hateful ones, and she hated them.

"Erin?"

She looked up, realizing that the waiter had departed and that Keith was gazing at her with his enigmatic eyes, his face revealing nothing of his thoughts. He wouldn't give an inch, she mused vaguely, not an inch. He wouldn't offer bedroom lies or empty promises. He was hard, paradoxical, uncompromising, secretive, angry— and altogether dangerous.

If she had a grain of sense, Erin realized, she would walk away from him and never look back. Instead, she heard herself say evenly, "Your terms. Which are?"

"Which are brutally unfair." His voice was still quiet and matter of fact. "My work comes first,

Erin. It has to. And you aren't involved in it. No questions. And no ties. I don't want a love affair. I don't want a relationship. I just want you. For as long as it lasts—and I don't know how long that will be. I can promise not to be cruel, but I can't promise to be kind. I can't say I won't hurt you, because I probably will."

Erin drew a deep breath, her eyes locked with his. "You are a bastard, aren't you?"

Four

"Sometimes." There was no apology in his deep voice. "Often, these days."

Erin took a swallow of her drink and wished she'd ordered something stronger. "You expect me to accept all this? Meekly agree to have a—what? A fling? Sleep with you because all you want from me is sex? Why should I agree to that, Keith?"

Very softly he said, "Because you want me too."

She didn't say another word. The lifelong training that had taught her to show her best face in public always and to keep her private emotions to herself served her well now. She wanted to hit Keith with something, to storm at him and rant and walk out. But the low hum of conversation all around them in the restaurant steadied her, and her social mask held. Just.

She wondered if he knew he should lay out his "terms" in a public place where she was unable to react as she wanted to. If so, that was as unfair as all the rest, because not being able to vent her emotions meant that her first negative impulses had to be fought and reined, and that gave her far too much time to become aware of other much deeper feelings.

When their food came, she ate as automatically as she'd ordered, and couldn't have said later what she had eaten. He was as silent as she, but she could feel his eyes on her almost continually, and she wondered what he was thinking.

That was the most difficult part of this entire situation, not knowing what was driving him. She could feel his emotions sometimes, so intense they were almost shocking, but his thoughts were a puzzle to her. She believed what he had told her was honest—but not the whole truth. This mysterious "work" of his was the most important thing in his life right now, and whatever it was, he had no intention of telling her anything at all about it. His terms made it clear. He could—and certainly wanted to—share his bed with her, but everything else was off limits. No promises at all.

It should have been easy to say no, Erin thought miserably, confronted by her own confusion and uncertainty. Few women would have hesitated when presented with such unjust conditions, not if they valued their self-respect. And she *did.* But it wasn't easy at all to allow the hurt and indignation to voice a flat refusal.

For the first time in her life, Erin began to understand how some people could be carried so far from reason, from logic and sense, when emotions drove them. Because that was it. No matter what her mind told her, her emotions tugged her wildly in the opposite direction. Even knowing that she had precious little chance of emerging from this unscathed, she wanted whatever she could get from Keith, and the realization was as terrifying as it was humiliating.

And it made her angry. Angry at him and angry at herself. What was wrong with her? Why couldn't she treat his proposition with the contempt it deserved?

Because it hurts him too.

Erin examined this sudden, new idea, and realized it was more than just a wistful hope. All this time, she'd been listening to more than his words; that was why his anger hadn't frightened her, and why she'd been so confused by what he was telling her. Despite his curt recitation of terms, Keith was deeply disturbed by his own feelings for her, and hated making the proposition both because he knew the unfairness of it and because *it wasn't what he wanted.*

But he wanted her. The desire that had exploded between them had overwhelmed him just as much as it had her.

She had heard that in his voice, heard it in the subtle shades and nuances she had learned to listen to in her father's world. All her instincts told her that although he was clearly obsessed with this work of his, he was also obsessed with her.

Erin didn't know what that would lead to. Perhaps nothing. Even if she agreed to his proposition . . . especially if she did. Perhaps all he needed was to let the passion run its course, to get her out of his system in the most basic and simple way possible—by taking her to his bed. But would that be the result if they became lovers? Could he allow her to know him in the most intimate of ways without also exposing other parts of himself to her—even if he didn't want to?

And what about her? Could she risk so much, gamble her self-respect, possibly even her future, on the chance there was more between them than passion?

What did *she* want? Only an affair, a chance to explore desire she had never felt before? Or had this tenuous bond she sensed between them tied her to him in ways she hadn't begun to understand? That connection she thought, had been forged in the dawn hush of nameless, faceless conversations, when a much more gentle Keith had spoken quietly and perceptively. No masks were needed in the darkness. The man he really was revealed himself only in those talks at dawn.

But that door had begun closing the moment they saw each other in the brightness of day, shutting firmly by the end of their breakfast together, and Keith clearly had no intention of opening it again. Could she? Could she find the source of his pain and anger even if he didn't want her to?

Totally wrapped up in her thoughts, Erin was only dimly aware of finishing the meal, and didn't notice when Keith refused coffee or dessert for them both and signed the check.

"Will you walk with me on the beach?"

She looked at him, nodded slowly. So many questions, she thought, and the path to answers so potentially painful.

Erin remained silent while they walked without touching back through the lobby and took the path to the beach. She paused when they reached the sand to step out of her shoes, and carried them along with her small clutch purse in one hand. The tide was out and turning, and they walked on the hard-packed sand that would be covered with water later. The moon was rising, hanging low and full over the ocean, and the beach was deserted.

"You haven't said a word," Keith said finally, reaching up to loosen his tie with a jerky movement that belied the calm tone of his voice.

"What can I say?" Her voice was just loud enough to rise above the steady roar of the ocean. "You've stated your terms very frankly. I suppose I should be grateful for that; at least I know where I'll stand if I don't leave."

"You're mad as hell, aren't you?"

She stopped and turned, looking up at his face and glad the moonlight was behind her. "Shouldn't I be? You won't even try to pretend, will you, Keith?"

"Pretend what?"

"That you care about me." She didn't want him to pretend, but she wanted to hear what he had to say in response.

"Is that what you want? Pretense? I told you I wasn't playing games, and I meant it, Erin."

"So all you're offering is lust?"

He made a slight movement as if he would have reached out to her, then slid his hands into his pockets. "I want to be with you," he said flatly. "When I can, as often as I can. I want to hear your voice and look into your eyes. I want to touch you, make love to you. If that's lust—then so be it."

Erin wished he would touch her now. There weren't any questions when he touched her. "Make love? That's a euphemistic way of putting it, don't you think? It hardly describes what two people do when they aren't lovers, aren't emotionally involved with each other, aren't having an affair. They share nothing but a bed. There are better words for that. Ugly words." She was quite deliberately needling him, hoping for some kind of reaction that would prove her instincts about him were right.

"Don't." The word seemed to come from somewhere deep in his chest with a guttural sound. "Don't say it. Don't think it. If I were looking for nothing but cheap sex I wouldn't come to you, Erin. I don't want only a warm body in my bed, a carnal pill to make it easier for me to sleep. If that's what you believe, then get on the plane tomorrow."

"I don't know what I believe," she told him, more than a little fierceness creeping into her voice. "More than sex—and less than an affair? What is that? Does it have a name?"

"Want," he said roughly. "Need. That's all I have to offer you."

Staring up at a face that stark moonlight painted even harsher and more compelling than normal, Erin wondered suddenly why he didn't touch her, hold her, why he didn't take advantage of a desire they both knew she couldn't handle. If the answer was that he refused to try and sway her in a way she couldn't fight, it did great credit to him as an honest man. And added another layer to his complex personality to baffle her even more.

Erin was a normal woman, and she had dreamed the normal dreams a woman's heart knows. She had thought of love, of moonlight and roses and a deep voice saying magical things to stir her heart and her blood. She had dreamed of a faceless lover who wanted only her, who was her match and her mate on some basic level they both recognized.

Keith had sent her roses, and the moonlight was streaming over them both. But. . . . The words his dark voice uttered were blunt and stark, and even though they stirred her blood, they also made her heart ache. And perhaps Keith did want only her, but not forever, only for now.

How could she love a man who—

Erin caught her breath, everything inside her hanging suspended for an endless moment. Then, before she could blurt out something he certainly wouldn't want to hear, she turned abruptly and hurried back toward the hotel, almost running.

He didn't call after her. Or follow her.

Julia looked up from her comfortable chair in the corner of the lobby and watched an elegantly dressed and astonishingly beautiful young woman hurry across the marble floor barefoot, her shoes and purse clutched in one hand, her bright red hair windblown, and her face unnaturally pale. After watching the young woman disappear into one of the elevators, Julia returned her gaze to the very large man sitting beside her, and said, "That doesn't look promising."

Cyrus Fortune, who had also keenly observed Erin's entrance, shook his head a little. "They aren't having an easy time of it. He doesn't dare tell her why he's here, and she's left with nothing to hold onto. Not even a promise."

"Why not a promise, Cy? Every woman needs that, even if it's an empty one."

"It isn't in him to make empty promises, my sweet." Cyrus smiled at his own delicate and lovely lady, his wise dark eyes unshuttered for her. Only for her. "He believes it would hurt her less if he prevents her from caring about him."

"He's wrong," Julia said.

"Yes. But he'll have to discover it for himself. And he'll have to discover he can't hide from her, not for long. She's too close."

"And he's afraid of closeness?"

His smile dying, Cyrus said, "He has reason. The sword over his head can endanger them both. If he makes a single mistake, speaks one wrong word, the men he's after will kill him. He doesn't want that part of his life to touch her, doesn't want that peril threatening her."

A bit hesitantly, Julia said, "Perhaps this isn't the right time for them."

Cyrus was smiling again, and his rich, powerful voice was tranquil. "It's the perfect time, sweet. Destiny commands. They are both at crossroads in their lives, where it was intended they should meet. All their experiences, particularly in the last year, have shaped them to face each other now."

"Can't we help?"

"We have. The connecting doors between their suites are unlocked."

Julia thought about that. "Such a little thing."

"No, sweet. An important thing. He must open the door from his side; she must open the door from her side."

She smiled slowly. "Fortune. A hypothetical guiding force, Did you know you were hypothetical, Cy?"

The white-haired, snowy-bearded, very old man looked so innocent that he would have deceived anyone. Except her. "Why, no, love, I didn't. I just like to meddle in other people's business, that's all."

During those girlhood daydreams when she had imagined falling in love, Erin had never considered doing so with the wrong man. He had always been a prince, naturally, untitled but the genuine article. And, of course, had adored her in return. Beyond that, he had laid claim to all the virtues a girl could want in her man, presenting her with an unscarred heart, a personality without complexities, and an unshadowed smile.

Only distantly aware of salt spray clinging to her and sand on her bare feet, Erin undressed and showered, then donned a silk nightgown and negligee. She sat on the edge of her bed and used her travel dryer on her wet hair, letting it dry wild because that was how she felt. She tried not to think, almost numb from the emotional battering of the day, but she couldn't stop the disjointed thoughts and feelings.

Keith was no bloodless fairy-tale prince born in a girl's uncomplicated heart. No innocent girl could ever have created him, or would have known what to do with him if she had. He was no man for a naive girl; there was too much of him, too much force, too much pain and anger, too many secrets.

But Erin wasn't naive or innocent, except in one strictly technical sense. The girl who had dreamed those chaste and simple dreams had grown into a woman well aware of the fact that men weren't princes. She knew happy endings weren't gifts, but something earned and never without a price. She even knew that sometimes a happy ending was beyond reach.

She knew.

The loud hum of the hair dryer died into silence, and she shook back her thick hair without caring what it looked like. Putting the dryer aside, she rose to her feet and wandered out into the dimly lighted sitting room. She didn't go near the balcony, but found herself gazing at those other doors, the ones that opened into his suite.

"Idiot," she murmured, her own voice startling

her a little in the silence of the room. "Don't be one. Just don't. So what if you love him? That's as mad as all the rest. The last thing he wants from you is love. He wouldn't even be kind, he said so."

But he wouldn't be cruel.

She tried to ignore the wistful little voice in her head, tried to convince herself that getting on the plane tomorrow would be the best thing she could do. He was shut away, and wouldn't open for her.

You could try.

What would she have when it was over? Scars on a part of her no one would see. Memories. She could, perhaps and in time, forget Keith, but if they were lovers, would she ever be able to forget him then?

Do you want to?

"No." She heard her voice, the instant denial, and knew it was true. She didn't want to forget Keith, no matter what the cost. And she couldn't walk away. She had to take the risk, had to take what he offered and gamble that she could build on it somehow.

Her decision made, the chaos in her mind settled down instantly. *Any decision is better than none*, she mused, remembering her father's oft-repeated words. It was a fleeting thought, because all her attention was focused on those closed double doors. Locked, probably; she knew they had been when she'd first arrived, because she had checked. Still, she squared her shoulders and walked over to them, putting one hand on the right doorknob and turning it.

Not locked.

On the point of drawing the door open, Erin hesitated. His side would be closed, and he had to open it. Which meant she'd have to knock.

What could she say to him? After she'd run from him so desperately on the beach, what could she possibly say? I changed my mind?

Unnerved, but refusing to let the hesitation throw her back into painful confusion, she drew the door open. At first, she thought his side was closed, but then she realized it was ajar a couple of inches. Was he so sure of her? Or had the maid simply been careless?

She was tired of questions, at least for today. Pushing his door open, she stepped quietly into his suite. There was a dim light coming from the bedroom, but he wasn't in that room. The balcony doors were standing open and he was out there, on the balcony, silhouetted in moonlight.

Her bridges burned behind her, Erin walked silently and steadily through the sitting room until she reached the open doorway. His back was to her and he was naked from the waist up, wearing sweatpants, barefoot like her.

"Keith?"

When he heard her voice, it was almost as if this long, tense day had never happened. Her sweet voice on a dark balcony . . . but the moonlight was bright, and it wasn't even midnight, and today had happened. Now he couldn't draw peace from her voice, because that was no longer enough. Instead, his heart hammered in his chest and it was hard to breathe evenly, and he wanted her so fiercely he could hardly bear it.

He turned slowly and saw her standing in the doorway, starkly beautiful in the moonlight, her bright hair painted dark but gleaming and tousled around her face. Her eyes were huge, colorless, like bottomless wells. She was dressed for bed. Dressed for him.

Keith didn't remember moving, but suddenly

he was standing before her, his hands lifting to her shoulders, and he didn't think he'd be able to let go of her this time.

"Are you sure?" he demanded, his voice harsh.

She didn't flinch from the sound, and her arms went up around his neck as she stepped closer. "I'm sure." It was hardly more than a whisper, but there was no uncertainty, and Keith had no will left to ask the question again.

It felt as if something had broken inside him, some restraining wall around the desire that had smoldered there since he'd first spoken to her. He bent slightly from the waist, both his arms wrapping around her, and when he straightened he had lifted her completely off her feet. He heard her catch her breath, and then his mouth covered hers and he heard only the hot roaring of his own blood in his veins.

Erin heard—felt—a pounding, but didn't know if it was her heart or his. Wrapped in his powerful arms and almost crushed against his immense chest, she felt so surrounded by him that they might have had only one heart between them. Her entire body seemed to soften and mold itself to his, all her senses responding wildly to the touch of him. And the taste of him. His mouth was hot and hard on hers, moving with a fierce, driven insistence that would have seduced a stone statue.

She wasn't made of stone. Her flesh was heating, yielding, her mouth opening eagerly to invite a deeper exploration, and she heard that strange sound again, that purr of pleasure vibrating in the back of her throat. He shuddered against her, his arms tightening almost convulsively, and then he lifted his head to draw a ragged breath.

She murmured a protest, her fingers twining in his thick hair as she tried to pull his head back down. But Keith was too impatient to be content with kisses. He shifted his hold on her and swung her up easily into his arms, leaving the balcony to stride toward his bedroom.

Erin hadn't been carried in her adult life, and she was surprised at the sensations. She wasn't a small woman, yet Keith's effortless power made her feel fragile. It was exciting and a little unnerving, and she couldn't seem to catch her breath.

He set her on her feet beside the turned-down bed, the lamp on the nightstand providing a warm glow that showed her his hard, intent expression clearly. She had never seen desire in a man's face, not like this, so potent and primitive and utterly male, and she was unprepared for the fiery jolt of her own senses in response. It made her knees go weak suddenly, all the strength rushing out of them, and she might have fallen if he hadn't been holding her.

But he was, his hands sliding down her back and curving over her bottom, holding her tightly against the pulsing fullness of his loins. A throbbing ache quivered through her, spreading outward from somewhere deep inside her shaking body, and she instinctively pressed herself closer because she knew only he could stop the tormenting pain. His mouth was moving over her throat, trailing fire, and she was already burning up, already so hot that she felt feverish and totally out of control.

It was almost frightening, the heat radiating from her, as if he had lighted a furnace somewhere in the depths of her and she couldn't contain the blaze, there was too much fuel. Her very flesh felt tight, almost hard, and so sensitized that even the pressure of her breasts against his chest was almost painful.

His hands slid up her back, tugging the negligee off her shoulders, and she had to remove her arms from around his neck long enough to shrug the silk to the floor. She could feel him gathering the silky skirt of her long nightgown in his hands, drawing it up, and she shivered when the cool air touched her heated skin. Then one of his hands curved over her naked bottom, the slightly rough texture of his palm sensuously abrasive on her skin, and another shiver of pleasure rippled through her.

A low groan burst from Keith, and he lifted his mouth from her throat and covered her lips. His tongue thrust deeply, met by soft touches of hers as she eagerly responded, and she was moving against him in a seeking way that made his desire spiral wildly to an intolerable pressure.

Erin could feel that, as if there were something inside him clawing to get out, and though it seemed impossible for her fire to burn hotter, what she felt in him added more fuel. She couldn't breathe, and her heart was pounding so fast and hard she knew it had to burst, it *had* to; it just wasn't possible for a heart to race so frantically and not explode from the effort. But she couldn't stop this, didn't want to, and she would have fought like a wildcat if anyone else had tried.

She wanted to say something when he finally ended that devastating kiss, to voice her astonishment or utter a plea she had no words for, or just to say his name, but all that would emerge was a soft sound she didn't even recognize, another unfamiliar sound of pleasure. Keith didn't wait for words. He drew the nightgown up over her head and tossed it carelessly aside, his brilliant violet eyes raking down her bare body with unshuttered hunger. Erin had never in her life stood naked before a man, but she was too dazed, too hungry herself, to feel embarrassment or self-consciousness.

And he gave her no time to ponder any of it, even if she'd been capable of it. With another rough sound, he lifted her and placed her on the bed, then rapidly stripped off his sweatpants. Then he paused there for just a moment, looking down at her as she stared at him dazedly, as if he realized she needed to.

Erin hadn't expected to be surprised by him, not really. In a broad sense, she knew what a naked man looked like; she had lived in many countries far less modest than America when it came to nudity, and with friends had visited more than one European nightclub famous—or infamous—for risqué acts. But technical, detached knowledge was one thing, and in no way prepared her for what she felt when she looked at him.

Until that moment, looking up at him from the bed, she had thought about only the emotional effects of becoming his lover. But it was impossible to gaze at his powerful body, gleaming bronze in the lamplight, and not think of the physical act. Her racing heart seemed to stop suddenly and then lurched once more into its impossible velocity, thudding madly in her chest. He was so big, so overwhelmingly, starkly male, his strength so vast that it made her vividly aware of what they were about to do and how vulnerable she was.

An imposing man clothed, he was most impressive naked, as if the trappings of civilization had no place on his powerful frame. There was none of the overdeveloped bulges that made weight lifters look so unnatural; Keith's hard body was packed with sinewy muscles that meant sheer, raw strength. Black hair covered his broad chest and arrowed down his flat stomach to the thicket over his loins, and her gaze clung there helplessly.

Her entire body responded vibrantly to his arousal, the fire in her burning even hotter. But a pang of sudden nervousness shot through her, mixed with several emotional realizations as different as they were disturbing.

Princes never took their clothes off, and dreamily chaste kisses didn't begin to even hint at the reality of passion. The passion of a man and a woman. But this was real. And it was a little scary. She was going to be closer to him than she'd ever been to anyone, take him inside her; bear his weight, and after that nothing could ever be the same.

For one fleeting instant, she wanted to beg him not to hurt her, wanted to warn him that she had never done this before, but then her eyes met the fierce heat in his and the words died unsaid. She wanted him, wanted this—and an intuitive certainty told her that he might stop even now, even if it half killed both of them, if she told him she was a virgin.

He had made this her choice. And she chose.

Unconsciously, she held one hand out to him, and his eyes flared savagely as he joined her on the bed. He kissed her, a deep and hungry kiss, one big hand touching her stomach and then sliding up over her ribs until it closed around her breast. Erin jerked, moaning into his mouth, her fingers digging into his shoulders convulsively. Her eyes remained closed, even when his mouth left hers to trail down her throat, because she felt so dizzy she knew the room would be spinning if she looked at it.

She was biting her lip, trying to hold back the sounds rising up from inside her, all her senses focused on what he was doing to her. His lips moved over her breastbone, then explored the satiny slope of one breast while his hand slowly stroked the other. She could feel his fingers kneading gently, and when his thumb lightly brushed her taut nipple the touch jolted through her like an electrical shock. She barely had time to gasp before his mouth clamped down on the other nipple, and that hot, wet caress wrung a cry from deep inside her.

The pleasure was so intense she thought she was going to shatter with it, so acute that it was actually painful. But it was a pain she endured helplessly, because her body was completely out of control, her senses raging wildly, the fire inside consuming her.

"Keith . . ." It was barely more than a whisper, a breath of aching sound.

Just his name, but he shuddered when he heard the husky sound of it and almost groaned aloud. As frantic as his own need was, the compulsive hunger for her was far more than an urgent desire to find release in the welcoming heat of her body. It was torture to hold back, to delay a completion his every screaming nerve demanded, but it was the sweetest torment he'd ever known. She was so responsive, and the varied textures of her slender body enticed all his senses to the point of madness. Her skin, heated with desire, was unbelievably soft and smooth, the firm muscles beneath supple and graceful. Her round breasts, flushed and swollen, filled his hands perfectly, and her tight coral-colored nipples almost pulsed in his mouth.

He wanted it to last forever, but his entire body was so tense that it ached intolerably, all his muscles rigid with strain, and he knew if he delayed much longer he'd go out of his mind. Still, the need to go on touching her had to be satisfied, and he lifted his head to gaze down at her as his hand slid over her quivering stomach.

"Look at me," he whispered harshly, anything approaching a normal voice beyond him.

Her eyes opened, darkened to emerald and dazed in her softly flushed face. Her hands moved to his neck and locked there, trying to pull him back down to her breast, and she murmured wordlessly. He resisted, wanting to see her face when he touched her, when his seeking fingers found the silky hair at the base of her belly. Her eyes widened, locked with his, and a gasp escaped her parted lips when he touched her. She was tense for a moment, but then her thighs relaxed and her eyes went sleepy, and a faint little sound purred in her throat.

That sound . . . that throbbing little sound made him crazy. It seemed to flicker over his senses like a brush of fire and caused his heart to lurch. He bit back a groan, clamping his teeth together so hard his jaw ached, his fingers slowly probing her damp, swollen flesh, stroking the most exquisitely sensitive nerves in her body.

Erin cried out softly, her body shuddering, and there was a look almost of panic in her eyes. "Don't," she whispered raggedly. "I can't—"

"Shh." He kissed her, over and over, his touch driving her relentlessly toward an unfamiliar brink until she was almost sobbing. When he finally widened her legs gently and rose above her to slip between them, she could only cradle his hard body helplessly.

She was so frantic by then that nothing could have shattered the spell of desire, but when she felt the sudden alien pressure, blunt and insistent, there was a split second of fear, as much of vulnerability as anything else. But she wanted this, wanted him, and nothing else was important. The fear vanished, pushed aside by her need for him, and all the starkly intimate sensations overwhelmed her.

Staring up at his intense, almost savage expression, lost in his burning eyes, Erin felt her body stretching slowly, opening for him. His throbbing flesh was a primitive male demand, and her own feverish need compelled her to surrender to it. To him. A twinge of pain caught at her breath as his entry was barred, and she saw the sudden darkening of his eyes the instant he realized the truth.

"Erin . . . " His voice was a hoarse rasp and his body shuddered violently as he fought for control.

Surely he couldn't stop *now?* Erin had a panicky notion that he could, convinced that his relentless will was equal to anything. And she wasn't about to give him time to think about it. She wreathed her arms around his neck and pulled herself up enough to kiss him, her legs lifting to wrap around his hips. All she knew of passion was what he had taught her, but that was enough, more than enough, for her to brand him now with her own fiery demand. If this was all he was willing to give her, she'd damned well take every bit of it she could get.

She felt as well as heard a growl from him that was probably an oath, wordless and fierce, and his instant's hesitation was no more than that. One of his hands slipped down between their bodies, touching her insistently, and she felt the burning pressure increase even as his caress guided her relentlessly to the edge of some peak that seemed just beyond her reach.

She couldn't believe what he was making her

feel. It was maddening, a hot, breathless tension so sharp-edged it was as if a living thing were trying to escape from the core of her. Then she felt a sudden sharp pain as something gave way, and for a shocked instant she was conscious of nothing except the incredible sensation of his flesh throbbing deep inside her.

He was kissing her almost wildly, and when the moment of shock passed she realized her body was still quivering on the edge of something. Her hands were compulsively stroking his back and shoulders, and she instinctively lifted her hips a little to take more of him when his body settled fully into the cradle of hers. The small movement yanked a groan from Keith, and he immediately began moving slowly inside her.

She realized he was being careful, even though the strain on his face and in the rigid muscles of his arms and back made it clear how difficult it was for him to rein himself. Erin wanted to tell him not to do so, not to hold back for her sake because there was no pain now, but then his hand was on her again and the spiraling tension edged into a new kind of pain. It was winding tighter and tighter around her, wringing a moan from her throat, making her writhe because it was too much and she couldn't bear it anymore.

If she'd had the breath to say anything at all, she would have begged him to stop. But then, just when she knew that another second of the exquisite tension would kill her, something snapped violently and everything inside her seemed to melt until she was nothing but a hot, pulsing, liquid pool of pleasure. She heard primitive sounds and sobs escaping her throat, and she heard the hoarse cry of Keith's pleasure as his powerful body shuddered in her arms.

Five

Erin wasn't thinking very much about questions. She had never in her life felt so utterly limp and boneless, almost floating even beneath his considerable weight. He was heavy, but she wasn't the least bit uncomfortable; in fact, she felt wonderful. Her arms were wrapped around his neck, her legs coiled with his, and she didn't want either of them to move. His forearms were underneath her shoulders, his fingers moving in her hair, and once her own breath steadied she could feel the warmth of his against her neck. She wanted to go to sleep just like this.

Keith, however, was obviously thinking of questions. He lifted his head to gaze down at her, his vivid eyes still darkened to purple. He kissed her, almost as if he couldn't help himself, but his voice was strangely flat when he spoke.

"Why didn't you tell me?"

"You didn't ask," Erin murmured.

A frown drew his flying brows together. "Dammit, Erin, it never occurred to me! You can't tell me you haven't had men chasing you since you hit puberty."

She had to smile a little, curiously undisturbed by both his anger and the conversation. "As a matter of fact, I can tell you that. Men don't chase me, Keith."

"Maybe you have another name for it," he said, obviously disbelieving her statement.

Erin shook her head slightly. "They don't. Never have. Oh, sure, they ask me out. Talk to me. Dance with me. But most of them don't make passes. I don't know, maybe I didn't want them to, and they sensed it. Or maybe . . ."

He was watching her intently, and when her voice trailed off, he prompted, "Maybe what?"

She hesitated, then said slowly, "I've always felt like an ornament. Something pretty a man likes to wear on his arm. I guess men don't think about taking an ornament to bed."

"Is that how you think I see you?" Keith demanded. "As an ornament?"

"No." Her reply was instant and certain. "I'm not sure how you see me, but I know it isn't that way."

After a moment, and clearly choosing to ignore the implied question, Keith said roughly, "You should have told me, Erin. Do you think I would have let things go so far if I'd known you were a virgin?"

"No, I think you would have put me on the plane." She met his gaze steadily. "But it was my choice, Keith. You made it mine when you offered your terms—and I accepted them."

"How can you know what you've accepted if you've never been in a man's bed before?"

She managed a little laugh. "Physically inno-cent is one thing, but I doubt it's possible to be completely innocent. Not in today's world, or at my age. I know what I'm doing. I understood your terms."

"Then why did you accept them?" His voice was still flat, hard, but there was anger underneath the control.

Erin wasn't surprised by it. Anger was, at least at this point in his life, so much a part of him that it helped fuel almost every other emotion. She thought he was angry at himself more than her, but in any case she wasn't disturbed by it. In fact, she had an idea that the force of his emotions, often contained but seldom hidden, was one of the reasons she was in his bed now. His emotions had freed hers.

The men of her father's world were always . . . civilized. They moved in houses of government and diplomatic enclaves with their elegant manners and quiet voices and subtle words, and no matter what it was they were saying they always meant something else. Each of those men was habitually elusive and evasive and so calculating that the real man seemed a pale ghost overlaid with deception.

But not Keith. He was secretive, yes, but not subtle. What he said was forthright and blunt, and his emotions were so intense she could literally feel them. She thought she could trust her instincts where he was concerned, believed that no matter how contradictory he might seem, she would always know at least a part of what he was feeling. She believed Keith didn't play games. The certainty of it was almost as reassuring as words of commitment would have been.

"Erin?"

She blinked, realized he was waiting for an answer to his question. She couldn't tell him the truth. He didn't want her love, and she wouldn't offer what wasn't wanted. Finally, she said steadily, "You didn't see an ornament. I like being treated like a woman, Keith. That's reason enough."

He looked at her broodingly, one hand lifting to brush a strand of fiery hair away from her face, his fingers lingering to trace her cheekbone. "Is it?"

She smiled at him, determined to keep his terms firmly in mind no matter what it cost her. "I think so. It's a wonderful feeling, being desired. I've never felt this way before. And I never knew—this—was so exciting. You're a wonderful lover, Keith." Then her smile wavered slightly. "Do you mind if I call you that? A lover?"

His facial muscles tightened. "No."

"I couldn't think of a better word," she confessed. "I know it's euphemistic, but—"

Keith bent his head and kissed her, a bit roughly. She had the vague impression that he'd done it primarily to stop her from saying any more, but she didn't think very much about his reasons. That kiss, hard and curiously possessive, felt like a brand, and sharp excitement quivered in her when she became aware of his renewing desire. Her own body had been faintly, languorously throbbing during their entire conversation, and now the pulsation grew stronger, faster.

He muttered something against her mouth and then lifted his head, looking down at her with what was almost a glare. "Dammit," he said thickly, "I want to keep at you until neither of us can walk without help."

Erin drew a shaky breath. "That—sounds fine to me," she murmured.

"It isn't fine," he said in the same tone, kissing

one corner of her mouth. "You'll be sore. I shouldn't—"

"I don't care." Her fingers probed the tensing muscles of his back and shoulders. "I don't feel sore. All I feel is you."

The bold invitation in her voice wasn't something he could ignore, especially when her body clasped his with tight heat and she moved under him with an innate sensuality that stole his breath and what little control he could claim. Her innocence had shocked him at some deep level, jolting his emotions as well as his senses. Disquiet was still very much with him even though he couldn't define it. But desire swept even that aside. He wanted her again, even more wildly than before, and the power of his desire sent his disturbing tangle of emotions flying.

She was astonishingly uninhibited, her passion so sweet and giving it drove his higher, her response so total that she went to his head like some fine, rare wine. Everything about her, from the texture of her skin and the misty depths of her eyes to the kittenlike sounds she made in passion, aroused him to heights he'd never known before. It was like a compulsion, loving her, a desperate, greedy, savage hunger that had to be satisfied no matter what it cost him.

During those intense moments, nothing else mattered. If he realized the primitive emotions could never have sprung only from lust, and that his profound need for her, Erin, was an instinctive hunger for joining as well as a sexual one, he didn't think about it. He didn't think about anything except the hot, sweet torment of their passion.

Erin woke to the realization that she was alone.

She heard water running in the bathroom, and managed to pry her eyes open enough to see the clock on the nightstand. Two A.M. Well, she thought sleepily, he *was* accustomed to working nights. But she wasn't. A long, tense day had culminated in a very active evening, and she was so blissfully weary she didn't want to move.

She was in the middle of the bed, the covers drawn up over her limp, naked body. Partially awake now, she was conscious of that wonderful pulsing sensation deep inside her, and she wanted to purr with contentment.

After the emotional upheaval of the day, she couldn't help but be a little amused at herself, because she should have been at least slightly worried—and she wasn't. Maybe that would come, but it hadn't yet. Any sensible woman, she decided drowsily, would be worried. But then, any sensible woman wouldn't have become the mistress of an angry man by midnight of the day she'd first seen him.

Her first lover. A man who refused ties, promises, or even questions, who had offered a proposition rather than a proposal, and who had taught her to feel a passion so great that the memory of it now was still able to take her breath away. The man who was a few feet away in the bathroom, the man who had been shaken by her virginity and who was still, she thought, disturbed by it. The man who felt so *much* on so many complicated levels she might never get to the bottom of him even if he gave her the time to try. The man she loved.

She thought she should have been appalled, but drifted back to sleep without bothering to worry about it.

Her next sensation was of coolness as the covers were drawn away, and then strong arms gathering her up easily. She loved that, being carried by him, and murmured her pleasure. The next thing she knew, she was immersed in warm bathwater just the right temperature with bubbles up to her chin. She opened her eyes and stared at what little she could see of herself, vaguely aware that he had bundled her thick hair behind her head so that it formed a comfortable cushion on the rim of the tub.

This resort hotel supplied numerous amenities for its guests, including bubble bath for the deep, oval tubs that were the essence of comfort. Erin was comfortable—and slightly bemused.

There were several lights in the bathroom; he had turned on only one so that the illumination was soft rather than sharp. She looked up at Keith as he knelt by the tub, searching for words in the haze of contentment and finally settling for, "Why am I here?"

His mouth curved in a slight smile, though his eyes remained darkened and intent. "You may not feel it now, but you will in the morning. Any new—activity—uses muscles you didn't know you had."

Erin stretched out her legs and winced slightly as the muscles of her thighs twinged. "You could be right," she admitted, recalling her childhood days on horseback, when a ride after months out of the saddle had left her stiff and sore.

That thought led to another along the same lines, as she remembered a favorite theory of one of her teachers. He had maintained that the attraction of adolescent girls for horses had a sexual base. Many of the muscles used in riding were the same ones exercised by sexual activity, and the symbolism of gripping a powerful animal between the legs, he said, was rather obvious. It was a "safe" outlet for sensations and emotions with which an immature mind hadn't learned to cope.

After hearing that, Erin had stayed away from her horse for weeks, feeling ridiculously guilty about her affection for him. Him! She *would* have had to own a gelding! She wondered, now, how many of her classmates had been as unnecessarily upset as she'd been. That teacher had either been thoughtless or perversely cruel to have put those ideas into the minds of young girls, so many of whom had owned horses.

"Is the water too hot?" Keith asked.

She could feel the heat in her face. "No, it's just right."

"Then you're blushing. Why?"

Erin eyed him, and decided to keep her memories to herself. "I haven't been put into a bath since I was seven. And never when I was sound asleep." He had told her he couldn't promise he'd be kind, but this was kind, she thought.

His smile remained, and he seemed to hesitate before he said dryly, "If I'd lain there any longer and watched you sleep, you would have had even more reason for aching muscles in the morning."

Accustomed to graceful compliments and flowery words, Erin found his bluntness curiously refreshing. And she wasn't at all embarrassed by it.

"You watched me sleep?" she ventured, far more disturbed by that.

Keith nodded, but didn't elaborate. Instead, he reached out and down, finding her lower thigh beneath the bubbles and beginning to gently massage it. Erin had experienced the expert touch of a masseur in some of the finest spas in Europe, but nothing compared to the melting, boneless sensation that swept over her as Keith's fingers slowly kneaded her muscles. She actually wanted to whimper out loud with the pleasure of it.

Her eyelids grew heavy as weariness vanished, and between her lashes she stared at his arm, starkly bronze against the white bubbles. The heat of the water was seeping into all her other muscles, and both his hands were on her thighs now, massaging slowly and deeply. She was turning to jelly. Quivering jelly, because the touch of his hands was as sensual as it was relaxing.

Her veiled gaze moved up over his forearms, lingered on the pulsing movements of his biceps, then his shoulders, and finally his face. He was looking down at the bubbles that hid the body he was touching, his expression taut and eyes narrowed. She loved that look. It was fierce and hard, primitive in a way that touched some cord deep inside her.

Maybe that was it indeed, she thought dimly. The reason. He was unlike any other man she'd ever known, and the vitality in him, the intensity was so strong and honest, it touched a part of her no one else had even come close to. When he was like this, his hands on her, it was as if her whole body understood an immutable truth that her mind was accepting only now. She was his. She was connected to him, belonged to him, on some instinctive, ancient level where language was only emotion.

Erin made a soft, almost inaudible sound, and his hands stilled as he looked at her face. Then, without a word, he reached for the bar of soap lying on a ledge near the faucet. She hadn't been aware of the passage of time, but realized now that the bubbles had begun dissolving and that the water had cooled to lukewarm. She didn't want to move. Her skin tingled warmly from the heat of the bath and his touch, and though she thought she should probably protest his obvious intention to bathe her because it didn't seem quite right that he should do it, she couldn't summon the energy.

Keith flipped the lever that would slowly drain the water from the tub, then worked up a lather in his hands and set the soap aside. Beginning with her slender feet, he slowly worked his way up her legs, caressing and massaging more than anything else. He had meant this interlude to be relaxing, but should have known, he acknowledged silently, that he couldn't have his hands on her without going crazy.

A tall woman, she was so perfectly proportioned that her body was almost delicate. And she was revealed to him slowly as the water around her drained away, her golden flesh glistening in the soft light. He couldn't take his eyes off her, and his hands were reveling in the slippery exploration. He stroked the slick lather from her feet to her chin, moving so slowly that he was torturing himself. He saw her breathing quicken, watched her nipples tighten as his hands swirled the soapy foam around them, felt her stomach quiver and contract beneath his touch.

His heart was pounding so heavily that his chest ached, and when she made a soft little sound as his fingers slid between her legs, his own desire ran like fire through his body. He felt as if he was being taken apart, cell by cell, and wouldn't be whole again until he lost himself in her, surrounded himself with the warmth of her. He retained just enough control to reach for the hand-held shower attachment and turn it on, waiting seconds for the water to reach the right temperature. Then he began rinsing the soap off her rosy body.

He heard her murmur his name, her sweet voice husky with desire, and wondered dimly how such a simple sound could affect him so powerfully. It was like being touched by a live wire, an electrical current shooting through him. He wondered it he really was going out of his mind.

He didn't care.

The instant the last of the soap swirled down the drain, he turned the water off and lifted her out of the tub, setting her on her feet on the mat and reaching for a towel. He dried her warm body blindly, because his mouth was on hers, and he probably missed a few spots because he was in a hurry, but she didn't utter a word of complaint as he carried her to their bed.

Erin opened her eyes slowly, reluctant to abandon a very pleasant dream but nagged by the internal clock that told her she had overslept. She was curled up against Keith's hard body with her cheek resting on his chest, and both his arms were around her. She liked that. A lot. Sunlight flooded into the room through the large window, and the covers were drawn up around them snugly. Only the soft hum of the air conditioning disturbed the peaceful quiet.

Content to lie in his arms no matter what time it was, she found herself thinking again that she should be shocked by all this. Or worried. At least mildly. It didn't seem quite decent not to be.

Odd the way one's upbringing prodded the conscience. Her mother, raised in a somewhat strict and socially visible family and married young to a British nobleman of frightening intelligence and cool manners, had depended a great deal on the conventions. She had clung to them because the rules were ironclad, unchanging in a world where so much else seemed to change from one day to the next. If anything, her husband's position and career had imposed an even stricter set of rules, where appearance was terribly important and doing the "correct" thing was at all times demanded. Erin's mother had lived by those rules.

Too young during the sixties to notice the whole world was rebelling, Erin had listened to her mother and, later, to the teachers who had sometimes taught manners and morals along with more academic subjects. And all of it, she realized now, might well be another reason she had so dutifully complied with her father's wishes these last years. Daughters were supposed to obey their fathers.

But Erin, unlike her gentle, soft-spoken mother, hadn't believed in all the rules—she had simply accepted them, she knew now. If it were otherwise, she'd be shocked to her bones for having broken most of them.

She wasn't very worried about it, just dimly bothered. Right or wrong, what she felt in Keith's arms was too wonderful to be a mistake. No matter how it ended, she had no regrets.

Needing, suddenly, to look at his face, she worked an elbow underneath herself and raised up. His eyes opened almost immediately, very vivid as they met hers.

"Hello," she said solemnly. He didn't look sleepy at all, and she realized he'd been lying here awake just as she had.

Curling one hand around the nape of her neck, Keith drew her toward him far enough to kiss her thoroughly. "Hello," he murmured when he could, gazing at her beautiful face with an unconscious fascination. There was something different about her, something he sensed as well as saw. After their night together she was more . . . vibrant, more alive. As if a gauzy veil had been stripped away, leaving her fresh and bright and new,

"Do you realize it's after eight o'clock?" she said after glancing over at the nightstand. "I haven't slept this late since I was a child."

"You had a busy night," he said, and felt his heart lurch when her lips curved in a smile so intimate it was like an actual physical caress.

"Yes, we did, didn't we? Did you wake me up around dawn? I think I remember that."

"You'd better remember it," he growled, the memory vivid in his own mind. A new experience, making love to her in the darkness, only touch guiding them.

"You're insatiable," she said, then added musingly but in a faintly pleased tone, "And so am I. It's disgraceful."

Even though she had been totally responsive since the first time he had touched her, and had shown not a single flicker of embarrassment, hesitation, or self-consciousness in all the hours since, he had half-expected some sign of withdrawal this morning. It was the traditional moment for doubts, regrets, and coolheaded reason to prevail, and since she had taken her first lover—on his definitely one-sided terms—the night before, it wouldn't have been surprising if the morning after had brought with it a hint of some distress.

But if she felt anything other than contentment in the situation, it didn't show. And, gazing into the bright depths of her green eyes, he knew that she *was* content. Instead of reassuring him, the knowledge made him more afraid than ever he was going to hurt her.

"You're looking fierce," she said consideringly. "What's wrong, Keith?"

"Nothing," he said, because it was too late to stop this. He knew damned well he couldn't stay away from her now if somebody held a knife to his throat. Hell, he hadn't been able to let three or four hours pass without needing her so wildly it was like insanity. Keeping his voice steady, he added, "Except that neither one of us has been very sensible. We should have taken precautions."

"I didn't think about that," she admitted, "but it's all right. My periods got very erratic a few months ago, and my doctor put me on the pill. He said it was stress, and told me I needed a vacation." Her mouth curved in a smile. "I'm glad I didn't listen to him then."

He pulled her head down and kissed her again, angry at himself because his first impulse had been to tell her to throw the damned pills away. The thought of his child growing inside her was so seductive it made his throat ache. He had thought of having children before, the idle thoughts most men have at some point or other, but this—this was a grinding hunger that went deeper than his bones. A little girl with Erin's bright hair and sweet smile, or a boy with vivid green eyes. . . .

God, he *was* going crazy.

When he finally ended that deep kiss, she drew back only a little. Lying half on top of him now, her forearms resting on his chest, she touched his beard-stubbled jaw with gentle fingers and murmured, "So much anger. Such an angry man."

"I don't hide it very well, do I?" he managed with a short laugh.

"No. You hold it in, but you don't hide it."

He shifted his hand from the nape of her neck to her cheek. "It isn't because of you."

Her gaze was steady. "Part of it is."

"No—"

"Yes." She nodded. "Yes, it is. Because I'm here. Because I'm . . . a complication."

Had he made it so obvious, or was she perceptive enough to sense it? He didn't know. He wanted to hold her tightly and tell her this wasn't a mistake—but he couldn't be sure it wasn't. She didn't seem to expect reassurances, and that disturbed him more deeply than anything else.

"I'm also hungry," she finished in a lighter tone of voice. "As a matter of fact, I'm starving. Room service?"

"Fine with me."

"Will you call, or—" Erin pushed herself up as she spoke, and broke off with a wince as a number of muscles protested the movement.

"Told you," Keith said, only his concern for her keeping him from yanking her back down on top of him. She was half sitting on one hip, a hand braced on the mattress and the other resting on his stomach. The covers had fallen to her waist, leaving far too much of her naked for his peace of mind. She didn't even seem to be aware of the provocative pose.

Eyeing him with a slight frown belied by smiling eyes, she said, "Well, don't gloat about it. I'm just a little stiff, that's all. If it hadn't been for the bath, I'd probably be in far worse shape—"

Then she blinked. "I didn't dream the bath, did I?"

"No," he answered after clearing his throat. He didn't know whether to laugh or curse out loud when he realized that he'd mentally counted back less than three hours to the dawn interlude of lovemaking and then assured himself somewhat desperately that he could let at *least* three hours pass without losing control like some randy teenager. He didn't know where he was getting the energy or the stamina. She was glowing, her bright hair, her eyes, her skin, all radiant—and if she didn't take her warm hand off his stomach soon, he was going to lunge.

She did move her hand, turning a bit gingerly to slide from the bed on her side, and then rising with only faint stiffness. Utterly unself-conscious, she moved naked around the room, gathering up the nightgown and negligee he had so carelessly thrown aside last night.

Keith closed his eyes, listening to what she was saying but not trusting himself to watch her.

"If you'll call room service, I'll go take a hot shower. That should ease the stiffness. Really, they never said a *thing* about that in sex education classes, not a word about using muscles you never knew you had." There was a pause, and then she said in a different voice, "Well, no wonder you were looking at me so strangely."

He opened his eyes and stared at her. She was standing at the mirror hanging above a low bureau, one hand holding her discarded sleepwear and the other attempting to smooth her gloriously tumbled hair as she frowned at her reflection.

"I look like a wild woman," she said, an indignant sound to her voice. "You could have told me instead of giving me that pained stare."

If it hadn't been for her mildly offended tone, Keith might have given in to his baser instincts because she looked so sexy standing there naked he could hardly think of anything else. But humor helped him to keep a grip on himself.

"I don't know why you're feeling insulted," he said. "Most people look their worst first thing in the morning, but you couldn't look less than gorgeous without the help of a special effects expert. And if I did look pained, it was because I am *in* pain."

She turned her head toward him, the dissatisfaction with her appearance completely forgotten. "Are you? I'm sorry. Is there anything I can do?"

He met the total innocence of her gaze, and wondered how on earth she could be so unconscious of her effect on him after last night. And this morning. He couldn't even consider the question while he was looking at her, so he cleared his throat again and said, "Yes, there is something you can do. Go take your shower, while I order breakfast."

"But—"

"Erin," he said bluntly, "I woke you up twice during the night because I couldn't keep my hands off you. I'm hoping I can at least get through breakfast, for my own peace of mind. But it's very difficult with you standing there naked. Take your shower, please. And get dressed."

She looked very solemn, but there was a tiny smile in her eyes. A smile that was pleased and a little surprised and not at all shy. "What a nice thing for you to say."

He shut his eyes. "Erin . . ."

"All right, I'm going. Order lots of food, will you? I really am starving."

"Ummm." He kept his eyes closed until he felt rather than heard her leave the room. She had gone back to her own suite. It was several minutes before he could summon the will to get up and find the room-service menu, and then place their order. After that, he went into his bathroom to shave and shower, trying not to remember the two A.M. bath that had triggered a passion so fierce he'd been shaking with it.

It was new to him, such wild desire. He had always tended to be a temperamental man, his emotions strong and impulsive, but he'd never felt the intensity of passion Erin roused in him. He told himself it was because they were still new to each other. Scarcely twenty-four hours had passed since he had first seen her; it was natural for passion to burn hotter at first. He reminded himself that the unusual pressures he was under, the vital need to contain so much of what he was feeling, undoubtedly increased his sex drive along with everything else.

It made perfect sense.

But he didn't believe it. Any of it.

This was something else, something he hadn't counted on. In the last twenty-four hours, he had barely thought of anything except her, the strength of her appeal pushing even his obsession with justice out of his mind. It had required a stoic effort of concentration for him to think enough to insist on the terms that might keep her safe. He could barely tolerate being this far away from her now, and she hadn't been out of his sight for fifteen minutes.

What would happen tonight, when he had to leave her for hours? And tomorrow night, and the next? He had to concentrate on his role, play his part so perfectly that the men he was after would never suspect the truth. Could he even do it now? Could he put out of his mind this craving he had for her? Could he ignore, at least for hours, the memories of touching her and tasting her and losing himself in her?

Standing in the shower, Keith turned the water to lukewarm and then all the way to cold, trying to damp a fire that seemed unquenchable. It didn't work. By this point, he hadn't really expected it to.

His mind went back to an earlier question, and he wondered again how she could possibly be so unconscious of her effect on him. He knew it was true, though, because the innocence in her eyes couldn't lie. She had said it wasn't possible these days for anyone to be totally innocent, and maybe she was right. Unless one were locked away from, or totally unaware of, the world, naivete could hardly outlast childhood.

But physical innocence could, and emotional innocence.

Hers had.

Part of him loved that, loved her unshadowed and guileless pleasure in his arms. She was so innately sensual, so warm and sweet and giving. And there wasn't an inhibited bone in her body. From her unself-conscious nakedness to her eager passion and the bemused enjoyment when he had bathed her, she wore the brand-new hat of a lover as if born to it.

He began to understand why some cultures still put a premium on virginity; when an unawakened woman found pleasure with her first lover, there was nothing to mar the experience for either of them. No ghosts, no painful memories, no comparisons for good or bad. Never hurt by a lover, she had no expectation of it.

Even though he had warned her.

He didn't know, even now, why she had accepted his terms. Perhaps—though he found it incredible—he was the first man to make her aware of her own passion. In fact, he was almost sure of that. But was it her reason? Was she content now because she was getting exactly what she wanted: exciting passion without strings or promises? Was she proving something, not to her father, but to herself? Proving that she was indeed free to make her own choices?

Was her passion for him, or had he simply released it?

Keith turned the water off and got out of the shower, not happy with any of his thoughts. As much as his mind insisted there could be no commitment between them, a more primitive instinct demanded that he know for certain if Erin wanted him . . . or only his passion.

Six

Breakfast arrived about the time Keith finished dressing, and Erin came through the connecting door to say, "Perfect timing; the maid wants to do my room." Dressed in a casual denim skirt and pale blue, short-sleeved blouse, her hair loose but brushed into neat, burnished waves, she was radiant.

In reasonable command of himself now, Keith was able to say calmly, "She won't do mine until late afternoon. I made that request when I checked in. But tell her not to lock the connecting doors, will you?"

Erin went back into her suite, then reappeared a few moments later and pushed his side of the door closed so that they wouldn't be disturbed by the vacuum cleaner. "She looked more resigned and saddened than surprised. 'Lord, what fools these mortals be.' I hope you ordered fruit. I love fruit."

Amused, Keith gestured to the laden table near his balcony. "Lot's of it. Tell me, are you usually this talkative in the morning, or is today special?"

For the first time, Erin looked a bit self-conscious. "I'm always like this. It's probably why I talked to you so much out on the balcony before we really met. Dad tried to break me of it because he hates conversation at the breakfast table, but it was the only thing I could never do for him. Does it bother you? I know it's hell if you can't wake up before coffee and somebody's chattering at you—"

Keith pulled her into his arms and kissed her, shutting off the flow. His night-owl hours of late were imposed rather than chosen; he was by nature a morning person, wide awake once his eyes opened, so her morning persona wouldn't have bothered him even if he hadn't loved the sound of her voice.

"I don't mind," he said, ending the kiss sooner then he liked because he was determined to hold on to his marginal control. Her response, instant and shatteringly sweet, tested that determination to the limits. He kept an arm around her as he guided her to one of the chairs at the table, knowing that if he didn't put some distance between them, he'd lose his battle.

"Are you sure? Unless I'm upset about something, I talk almost nonstop for the first hour or so."

"It doesn't bother me." He poured coffee for them. "By the way, have you called your father? You haven't mentioned it."

"No, I haven't talked to him." She was serving herself from a large fruit plate, and didn't look up at him. "The message light on my phone was blinking when I went in to take a shower. He wants me to call him today. I think he still believes that if he can just find the right combination of words, I'll be on the next plane to London."

"Is he so good with words?" Keith asked, transferring food to his own plate, but watching her intently.

"Expert. He could talk a snake out of its skin."

"Interesting analogy."

She looked up at him, then smiled ruefully. "I suppose so. But apt. I've seen him deal with men who'd make your blood run cold, and never lose his smile."

Keith was too curious not to ask. "What does your father do?"

After a slight hesitation, Erin said, "He's an ambassador. Has been for thirty years."

"Ambassador to England?"

"For England. My mother was American, but Dad's British. I have a dual citizenship."

The news was unexpected, and it bothered Keith. He didn't much care what Erin's father did for a living, but when the public visibility of a nation's ambassador combined with the anxiety of a father, things could get tricky. If that father decided to cross the Atlantic in search of his erring daughter, it was entirely possible Keith would find himself in the middle of a most unwelcome spotlight. He tried to reassure himself on that point; the American press might not even notice the arrival of an English ambassador in this resort area. Unless . . .

"Your father isn't anything else, is he?"

"Like what?"

"Like titled."

Erin looked absurdly guilty. "He's an earl."

"Great," Keith muttered. "That makes you Lady Erin. And the American press loves titles."

"I don't use mine over here," she protested. "It's just a courtesy anyway."

"I'll bet your father uses his."

"Well, yes, but—" She broke off, frowning a little. "Are you worried that he might come here?"

Keith had known the first time he set eyes on Erin that it would be all too easy to tell her things, even things he didn't want her to know. But this . . . His hesitation was brief. "I really don't want any unusual attention right now, Erin. It could be a problem for me. Is he likely to come here?"

"I shouldn't think so. He has to take up a new post in a few weeks, so he'll be very busy. I've never seen him abandon his work for any reason. Even when Mother died, he just worked harder than ever."

"If he's worried about you . . ."

Erin couldn't imagine her father crossing the Atlantic just because of her, but said, "I'll call him later today and tell him I'll fly over in a week or so to talk; that should satisfy him." She studied Keith's face, then added very quietly, "He doesn't have to know you exist unless you want him to. I hadn't planned to tell him anything about us."

He had to look away from those luminous green eyes as he said, "Don't mention me. To anyone." Concentrating on eating, he tried to remind himself that all this was for the best. The only relationship he could have with Erin right now was a sexual one, and she had agreed to that. So why did he feel as if he were betraying her by insisting that his only place in her life was in her bed, and secretly at that?

Everything had seemed so simple before he met her. He had set himself on a course of action that all the anger and grief inside him had demanded, and nothing had distracted him from his goal. Until he heard a sweet voice on a dark balcony. He had needed that then, he knew, needed the connection to sanity that she had unknowingly provided. For a time, she had kept him balanced, prevented his rage from drawing him over the edge.

But now, with his anger still eating away at him, he was farther from the edge, nearer to her; he wasn't balanced anymore. He was divided, not just by the role, but by the new conflicts raging inside him. Part of him wanted to turn away from the obsession that had driven him for months, to release those bitter emotions and allow himself to begin healing; but he couldn't let go, he just couldn't. He wanted Erin even closer, not kept away by a wall of secrecy, but at the same time was afraid that the danger of his role would spill over onto her, and he didn't even want to tell her what he was doing because he was afraid it would horrify her.

He didn't want their relationship to be only sexual. He wanted to be her lover in every sense of the word, to give her as much as she gave him. But . . .

Keith violently shoved the thoughts away. He looked across the table at Erin, suddenly conscious of the silence and wondering if she was upset. She didn't seem to be; her expression was thoughtful as she ate, but not withdrawn or anxious. But she was silent, and he knew he had disturbed her contentment. He hated that.

Reaching for anything to recapture the earlier relaxed mood, he said, "So you grew up in the diplomatic corps."

Erin replied to that easily and readily, smiling a little as she sat back and sipped her coffee. "More or less. I was usually in school, here or in Europe, with only vacations and holidays spent with Mother and Dad."

"Sounds like a lonely life," he commented, watching her.

Musingly, she said, "Not really. I had friends and family scattered all over. I would have liked to be with Mother and Dad more, but I didn't feel particularly neglected. Probably because I was never emotionally close to either of them. Dad was wrapped up in his work; Mother was wrapped up in him and in the social life of an ambassador's wife."

"No siblings?"

"No. Mother had several miscarriages while I was growing up. They left her frail and depressed. She knew Dad was disappointed, even though I doubt he said anything about it. But he wanted a son. I always knew that. His title had been handed down in a direct line for five hundred years. Now it will go to a cousin."

"He won't remarry?"

Erin looked faintly surprised. "I've never even thought about that, and I've watched women chase him for years. He should remarry, for himself as well as the title. Maybe now that I won't be there to act as his hostess and make a home for him, he will. He likes his life to run smoothly."

After a moment, Keith said, "I don't think I'd like your father very much."

She smiled. "He isn't a cold man, not really. But he is reserved and a bit detached. I suppose he has to be. In his world, people never say what they mean in plain words, everything is subtle, even deceptive. It's gamesmanship with them. And he plays the game very well."

"Even with his daughter?"

"Not intentionally, I think. Not deliberately. We didn't know each other very well when Mother died and I left school to live with him, and I suppose he didn't really think of himself as a father. I tried to make myself useful, and I believe I did, but I could never get close to him."

Her voice was quiet and matter of fact, but Keith thought he'd never heard anything so bleak as the simple phrase *we didn't know each other very well.* What a damning condemnation of any man! He told himself fiercely that if he were ever lucky enough to have a child, son or daughter, those words would never be said about him.

He cleared his throat. "Yet you were afraid you'd hurt him by breaking away."

"A euphemistic choice of words. Wishful thinking, maybe. I knew he'd be disappointed in me. I was even afraid that if I broke away I wouldn't have any place in his life at all. That I'd be dismissed from his mind. I suppose that was the real fear. That I could only be part of his life—" She broke off abruptly.

"On his terms," Keith finished evenly.

After a moment, Erin said, "I couldn't go on agreeing to his terms."

"What about mine?"

She wasn't sure what he wanted from her, what he wanted to hear. He had been clearly upset by the knowledge of what her father was, not because she was the daughter of a titled nobleman, but because that nobleman could direct unwanted attention at Keith and what he was doing here. She had done what she could to remove that worry.

But this . . . It was like walking a high wire with a gust of wind whipping around her, trying to maintain her balance when she couldn't predict where or when the next blast would come. His emotions were like that, escaping suddenly and without warning, triggered by something she said or did, and there was no way she could keep it from happening because she didn't know what it was that lay at the root of his simmering anger.

Erin didn't resent that, but it worried her for both their sakes. Their relationship was so tenuous because he had posted so many no trespassing signs, shutting off a great deal of himself from her. She had made up her mind not to ask for more than he was prepared to give her, yet she knew he was in pain and it went against both her nature and her love for him to do nothing at all to try and ease that.

"Erin?"

She lifted one hand in a helpless gesture. "What are you asking me?"

"I'm asking how long you can go on accepting my terms." His voice was flat in that familiar way that told her he was deeply disturbed.

Erin wouldn't have been human if she hadn't felt a flash of resentment—and she was very human. She was also, she reminded herself, dealing with a man who, where she was concerned at least, was so contradictory that it was maddening. He wanted no ties or promises, he said, and when she accepted his word, he had the nerve to ask how *long* she would accept it.

She took a deliberate sip of her cooling coffee, then said mildly, "Since you set the terms, why don't you set the time limit?" He looked a bit disconcerted, and she was glad.

"How can I?" he asked.

"How can I?" Erin met his gaze steadily. "Keith, you haven't given me any room to find that answer. I don't have the right to ask you anything at all, not about us. *You* defined what we are. And I think your words were 'as long as it lasts.' So I guess that's your answer."

He should have let it go then, but the part of Keith that needed to know if she wanted *him* was too strong and too primitive to fight. "My answer, yes. But not yours."

Erin looked at him for a long moment, her green eyes disturbed for the first time, a little wary and a little angry. She shook her head and tossed her napkin aside, then rose and went out onto the sunny balcony. Keith followed as far as the doorway, watching her as she looked out over the ocean. Then she turned back to him.

"You can't have everything your own way, Keith," she said in a voice that shook slightly. "I haven't asked anything of you. I haven't asked you to promise you'd be with me next year, or next week, or an hour from now. I haven't asked you to tell me where your anger came from, and why it's eating you up inside. I haven't asked you to cross the line *you* drew."

"I know," he said roughly. "I'm sorry."

"Then stop making it even harder for me. Stop making me feel like a damned sacrificial victim because you so obviously think I'm making a mistake. It was my decision, and I don't need you doubting that I know what I'm doing. I feel as if I'm walking through a mine field as it is."

"It doesn't show," he muttered. "I can't even tell if it's me you want, or just passion." He saw the flash of hurt in her lovely eyes, but her chin lifted swiftly, and her voice was very quiet.

"I won't make it any easier for you either."

"What are you talking about?"

"I'm talking about us. You want me, Keith, but you don't want me close emotionally. I've accepted that. But if you're off limits that way—so am I. You have no right to ask me *how long* I'll accept anything from you. Or even what it is I want from you. That wasn't part of the deal. You don't want a love affair, you don't even want a relationship, you just want me in your bed. I want the same thing, obviously. I haven't exactly tried to hide that from you. My reasons for agreeing, and my emotions about it, are none of your business."

It hurt, and he knew he deserved it. Because she was right. He had demanded that she forfeit every one of a lover's rights except for physical pleasure, and it was cruelly unfair for him to ask anything else of her at all.

He drew a deep breath, then took two steps and pulled her into his arms, holding her slender body hard against his. "Right now, all I can offer of myself is this," he said in a taut voice. "I don't have anything left to give you, Erin. Not now."

After a moment, her arms slid up around his neck, and she said almost gently, "When you do, if you do, then maybe we'll both have questions. But right now, this is enough for me, Keith. I don't want to think beyond it."

He didn't know if he believed her, but with her in his arms, he couldn't think beyond it himself. Whatever else he needed from her, physical desire was so potent that it pushed all else aside, and he didn't question that as he carried her back to their bed.

They left his suite only once that day, going for a walk on the beach while the maid was cleaning, and Keith realized that a part of Erin *was* quite deliberately off limits to him. Her earlier contentment had returned along with her casual ease, her eyes and smile unshadowed, but after their strained conversation he began to understand that she had marked the boundaries carefully and with precision. When he touched her, her response was totally honest, her pleasure unhidden; the label she had chosen to wear read *lover*, and she was as passionate and giving as any man could have wanted.

Conversation about them was matter of fact, focused totally on the here and now, and all emotions she revealed dealt strictly with the pleasure she found in his arms. Period. What she felt about him as a lover was obvious; what she felt about him as a man was her own secret. She readily answered his questions about her life, but asked none about him.

She never once crossed the line he had drawn.

Keith couldn't complain. He'd gotten what he demanded: Erin in his bed on his own terms. She didn't try to make him feel guilty about that, and she didn't indicate by the slightest sign that she wanted anything else from him. He should have been satisfied, but he wasn't. He managed to contain his struggle through the remainder of the day, but as evening approached his tension increased.

He had to leave her, had to put her out of his mind while he wore the skin of his alter ego, while he continued with his plan to destroy two men.

He barely let her out of his sight all day, a possessiveness that she seemed unconscious of, and when he literally forced himself to get ready to go, it was straight from their bed while she lay naked in a tangle of covers and watched him. He dressed casually in jeans and a knit shirt, knowing he had to stop at the boat and don a tuxedo; tonight he was attending a formal party at Vincent Arturo's palatial home, where he planned to begin drawing the threads of his plot tighter.

It would be a night of strain and tension, and he needed all his concentration.

He couldn't think of anything but her.

"You haven't called your father," he commented as he sat on the foot of the bed to put on his shoes.

Erin glanced at the clock on the nightstand; it was a quarter past six. "I'll call in a few minutes. He's always up until after midnight."

Keith stood up. He was ready, and he knew he couldn't delay any longer, but leaving her was killing him. He wanted to kiss her again, and hold her again. But he couldn't. Without moving toward her, he said, "Will you be here when I get back?" He meant here, in his bed, waiting for him.

"Yes," she said simply. Then, before he could turn away, she went on in a quiet voice. "Earlier today, you said that you didn't know if it was you I wanted or just passion."

"I had no right to ask that."

She half nodded, agreeing, but said gravely, "It's your passion I want. It's you I want."

Keith didn't ask why she was willing to tell him that, he couldn't have said a word right then. It meant more than he'd realized, too much for him to have an easy or ready response. He simply nodded, and left the room quickly.

Erin lay alone in the big bed for a long time, just thinking. The worries that had been absent this morning had finally arrived at some point, creeping into her thoughts from time to time all day. The kind of worries she'd expected. Not about what she had done; she loved Keith, and that was why she was in his bed now. That wasn't a mistake. But she was worried about him, and worried about the future. She had been able to push the anxieties aside while Keith was with her, but now that he was gone she couldn't ignore them any longer.

She thought it would have been easier if Keith had been content with his own terms. At least then, she would know exactly what was expected of her. But he was still holding her off with one hand while trying to pull her closer with the other, still immersed in a conflict she could sense, even feel sometimes, and yet didn't understand because he wouldn't talk about it with her. He didn't want her too close, and yet she wasn't close enough.

That was what gave her hope, as maddening as his contradictory desires were. Part of him *did* want an emotional closeness, she felt that with certainty—but he was fighting it.

It had been Keith's emotions she had trusted from the first because they were so strong she felt them and because she had known instinctively that they were honest. Now, after all the hours with him, she believed that even more. His physical desire, unhidden and almost shockingly intense, was a need for *her*, not merely a need for sexual release.

And she thought he cared about her, whether he knew it or would admit it. His vivid eyes, less enigmatic than they had been at first, held expressions she had read easily: burning hunger when he wanted her, pain when he had guessed the loneliness of her childhood despite her denial, anger when she had described her relationship with her father, and a wrenching reluctance when he had left her tonight.

He had said that all he could give her of himself was what his terms so briefly defined, that he had nothing left, but Erin didn't believe that. What she believed, what she felt with certainty, was

that he had built a wall with his anger, that simmering rage locked inside him, and until he
released that, it would continue to stand between
them.

But how could she help him free that fury? It
was all tied up with what he was doing here in
Miami Beach, she felt that. Something he had to
do; she no longer believed the fiction of "work."
He was here to do something very specific, something that put him under enormous pressure,
and whatever it was, he didn't want to tell her
because . . . Why?

With nothing more to go on, Erin couldn't
begin to answer that question. And she couldn't
ask him. She *couldn't*.

Her contentment since they had become lovers
was an instinctive thing; everything inside her
was certain that she and Keith belonged together,
and with such a certainty to hold on to, she could
live for today. But the connection between them,
strengthened during the last hours, also told her
that the conflicts in Keith, steadily intensifying,
could destroy him. And she didn't know how to
help him.

Deeply troubled, Erin got up and put on one of
his shirts that he'd worn earlier because it bore
his scent and she needed that feeling of his near-
ness. The last thing she wanted to do right now
was call her father, but she returned to her own
suite and placed the call, curling up on her bed
as she waited for him to answer.

Characteristically, almost his first words were,
"You weren't in your room this morning."

It was a question, and one she chose not to
answer. "Dad, I'm planning to fly over in a week
or two, before you leave for Turkey. We can talk
then."

There was a brief silence, only the faint hiss of the transatlantic connection audible, and then he spoke again in a very neutral tone. "You've met a man, haven't you?"

Was that his famed perception, she wondered, or did she sound different to him? It didn't really matter. Erin could have returned a flippant answer to his question, but their relationship had never contained banter—or any disrespect on her part. Her hesitation was brief. Keith had said not to mention him, but something, some intuition, told her that her father would be no threat to him.

Keeping her own voice neutral, she said, "Yes, I have."

"Is this man the reason you decided to remain in the States?"

The third degree, she thought, dispassionate enough to come from a diplomat. Not a father. "No. I decided that before I met him."

"Am I going to meet him?"

Honestly, Erin said, "I don't know, Dad. I'm not thinking past today."

There was another brief silence, and then his voice hardened. "A cheap affair, Erin? I thought I'd taught you better than that."

For the first time in their relationship, Erin didn't think about hurting or disappointing him, and all she felt was rage at his contemptuous dismissal. Her voice was shaking when she spoke, her fingers white on the receiver.

"What you taught me, Dad? I'll tell you what you taught me. You taught me that I had value to you only because of the way I look and the fact that men talk to me. You taught me to hide my own emotions, as if they were indecent somehow."

"Erin—"

"I'm not the son you wanted. I'm not an asset to your career. I'm not your secretary or your housekeeper or your hostess. And I'm not asking for your blessing, Dad, I don't even want to hear your opinion—"

"Erin." His voice was harsher than she'd ever heard it, so unexpected that it silenced her. He drew an audible breath. "I'm sorry if I offended you."

She stared across the room at nothing, thinking of the gulf that lay between them. Back in control, she said, "It doesn't matter. And if it relieves you to hear, my—affair—is a very private matter. Our fine, aristocratic linen won't be washed in public."

There was a pause. "You've never been sarcastic with me before," he noted quietly. "I've hurt you. I'm sorry. I didn't intend to do that. But this relationship is very sudden, Erin, and I wonder if you've given it enough thought."

Ever the diplomat, she thought, expressing a politely phrased question that really meant *are you out of your mind?* "That's my business, Dad. And his. I'm a grown woman; I'll make my own decisions, and my own mistakes."

This time the silence was much longer. When it came to father-daughter conversation, they really didn't have much to say to each other, Erin acknowledged sadly. And since she was far less hesitant in this conversation than ever before, her father had found no chink to subtly work his wiles on, no opening through which he could maneuver.

"Well," she said finally, "I'll see you in a week or so."

"Erin . . ."

"What is it?" she asked politely.

"Can this man take care of you?"

Knowing her father, he was probably asking if Keith was financially, socially, and/or politically prominent, not if he offered love and emotional support. But Erin supplied her own definition of the term "take care," and answered simply. "Yes, he can. I'll let you know when to expect me, Dad."

"Very well."

She cradled the receiver softly without saying good-bye, and remained there on her bed for a long time looking across the darkening room at an uninspiring print. If her father and Keith ever met, each probably would dislike the other and neither would ever understand the other. The only qualities they shared were strength of personality and intelligence, and each wore those traits so differently that they would provide no common ground.

Erin loved them both, and both men had set her at a distance; her father with detachment and Keith with an anger she didn't even understand. In a lifetime of trying, she hadn't been able to bridge the gulf of indifference between her and her father.

Unless she managed to close the distance between her and Keith, every instinct warned that she would lose him utterly.

He had asked how long she would be able to accept his terms, and now Erin knew the answer with certainty.

Not long. Not long at all.

* * *

It was almost three A.M. when a big, casually dressed man slipped into the hotel through a seldom-used side entrance, and across the street in a parked car two men watched as he disappeared into the building.

"Will he go through with it?" the man on the passenger side asked in a low voice.

The man behind the wheel had a hard face and shuttered eyes, and he lit a cigarette before replying. "I don't know. He was different tonight. Edgy, and I didn't like the look in his eyes. Like part of him was somewhere else."

The passenger, whose features were so bland he could have passed unnoticed through any crowd, didn't change expression. "What about Arturo and Wellman? Are they taking his bait?"

"Hook, line, and sinker. Wellman wants Arturo off his back so bad it's beginning to show, and thinks the cartel Donovan's supposed to be fronting for will get the job done. Arturo has his sights set on running this territory, and believes he'll have the cartel's backing if he launches a war against Martine."

The passenger gave a low whistle, then said musingly, "Pretty, isn't it? I have to hand it to Donovan; he's played those two sharks beautifully."

"The driver grunted. "Yeah, but he's way out on a limb. If his timing isn't perfect, he's going to get caught in the cross fire."

The passenger shot a glance at his companion. "You could have told Wellman that *Duncan* is the stepson of the man he asked Arturo to have killed more than a year ago. You could have stopped Donovan cold that way, or had him picked up."

"Don't remind me. It was a judgment call, and I still think I called it right. You know what that New York cop, the friend of Donovan's, told me.

He came back from Europe to bury his whole family, heard the cops tell him they *knew* damn well it was a hit but couldn't prove it, and the only justice he got was a closed investigation. He's hellbent on revenge, and I don't want to be the one who tries to stop him."

With a shrug, the passenger said, "Hey, I won't shed any tears over the likes of Arturo or Wellman, and if Martine gets a bloody nose, so much the better."

The driver grunted again. "Of course not. You're DEA, and a few less players in the war down here would suit you just fine. But I've been sitting on Wellman for more than a year, and I want to go through him to get Arturo's whole organization."

"Any luck?"

"Not till Donovan showed up. Since then, Wellman's been unusually chummy with Arturo, and he's been a bit careless. Donovan has them both convinced that his fictional cartel is the answer to all their problems."

Almost idly, the passenger said, "I don't suppose it's occurred to Wellman that the cartel, if it existed, would be a worse master than Arturo?"

"Hell, no. He didn't learn a damned thing from climbing into bed with Arturo. You'd think he'd see that he's just getting in deeper, but not him. He wants Arturo off his back, and he's completely convinced that the cartel, after killing to oblige him, would let him go his own way without asking anything of him but a few political favors."

"Donovan's got the nerve of a burglar," the passenger observed dryly. "He's told them two separate stories and counted on their mistrust to keep them from putting their heads together. And it's working."

"Yeah." The driver, his hard face expressionless, looked back toward the hotel. "But he's mad. He's mad as hell. And if it isn't over soon, he's going to blow up in all our faces."

Seven

When Keith slipped quietly into his dark bedroom, his first emotion was sheer relief. She was there, curled up in his bed deeply asleep. He could hear her soft breathing, and when his eyes adjusted he could see the dark gleam of her hair on the pillow and her curved shape under the covers.

It had occurred to him several hours ago that she might not be here, that despite saying she would, she could well have decided to fold her tent and leave. He didn't know what he would have done if she'd been gone, the fear of that had been haunting him. It had taken all he had, more than he'd ever needed before, to stick with his role, and all the time his heart had been thudding sickly in his chest and he'd felt cold through to his bones.

But she was here, and the relief of that was so great he almost groaned aloud with it. He wanted to rip off his clothes and crawl in beside her, hold her and make love to her. He wanted to wake her up the way he had yesterday and see the gleam of her catlike green eyes in the darkness.

But he couldn't join her just yet. He'd barely managed to force himself to stop and change at the apartment; he needed to shower away that other man, that other world. He was always conscious of the scents that clung to him, and he hated the stuff he used to slick back his hair and cover the silver. So, forcing patience, he undressed silently in the dark bedroom and then went into the bathroom, closed the door and turned on the light, being as quiet as he could. He took a quick shower, using no more time than necessary to get clean, then dried off hastily and returned to the bedroom.

Some distant part of his mind acknowledged the fact that sometime, and probably soon, he was going to reach the absolute limits of his energy and stamina, physically and emotionally. He could feel it even now, a raw sense of having pushed himself too hard for too long. There were too many strains and complications, too many emotions, too much tension.

But right now, he didn't care. Right now, nothing mattered except the fact that he needed Erin and she was here.

He slipped into bed beside her, finding her body naked and warm, hearing her contented murmur when he pulled her into his arms. He wanted to wake her up slowly as he had the morning before, to kiss her and caress her for long minutes while she gradually woke to the realization that she was being loved. But desire hit him with the force of a blow, his whole body shaking with it, and he knew he couldn't wait even a moment.

There was little patience left in him, but he managed to keep his touch gentle as he turned her onto her back. He pushed the covers away and eased her legs apart, then moved between them. He wanted to fuse their bodies together, to make her his so utterly that he'd never again feel that icy fear of losing her. And though his mind told him the future couldn't be mastered even by an iron will, all his deepest instincts and his overwhelming need for Erin insisted that he try.

Asleep, her warm, relaxed body welcomed his as if it recognized his touch, sheathing his flesh with a tight heat that drove his desire impossibly higher. She sighed and almost purred, the throaty sound sensuous, moving slightly and unconsciously to cradle his body more comfortably. She was so deeply asleep that she didn't wake even then, but she responded. He could feel the building heat and tension in her, feel the hardening points of her nipples against his chest, and the sleeping smile his lips touched was one he had watched in fascination during other passionate interludes.

She was dreaming. He realized that, and he didn't know if he was her dream lover. It was maddening to feel the heat of her response and yet know that she was unconscious of *him*, that her sleeping mind was immersed in an erotic dream triggered by physical sensations without identity. He couldn't stand it.

"Erin," he muttered hoarsely, pressing deeper inside her as his weight settled fully on her, his arms slipping under her, surrounding her. He kissed her fiercely, again and again, demanding that she know who was making love to her. And then he saw the gleam of her eyes in the darkness, heard her murmur his name and something else, something he wasn't quite sure he'd heard right, but that caused his emotions to surge so wildly he could barely contain them. Her mouth came alive beneath his and her body arched, her legs lifting to wrap around his hips as her arms went around his neck tightly.

All his thoughts scattered, swept away by raw need. It was like always when he touched her, when he felt the fire of her desire match his. Nothing else mattered but this, nothing except the woman in his arms and his shattering hunger for her. He couldn't get enough of her, even when she cried out and the tight clasp of her body caressed him in pulsing ripples of pleasure, he couldn't let go, couldn't let it end even for a moment, even for now. He kept her trembling body at the very peak, his own body so tense every muscle was quivering with the strain, driven by something so far beyond desire, so primitive and deep inside him, that its only name was necessity.

Until finally the limits were reached, breath gone, burning flesh and shuddering muscle pushed past endurance, all their raw senses shattering in a burst of pleasure so intense it edged into agony. The culmination left them both so utterly drained that they slept still entwined, bodies limp and sated.

Erin woke around seven, feeling so peculiar that for a few moments she lay with her eyes closed trying to define it. She was on top of Keith, she knew that; both his arms were wrapped around her and the covers were drawn up over their bodies. She didn't remember that, but he must have awakened at some point and managed to pull up the covers.

And physically, she felt . . . strange, but wonderful. Her entire body seemed to be tingling, and despite her memories of an exhaustion so absolute it had left her dazed, she felt energized now, filled with vitality.

Emotionally, she felt, for the first time, just a little bit embarrassed. She'd gone crazy, she remembered that. There had been an intensely erotic dream, Keith making love to her with wild hunger, and then it hadn't been a dream because it was real. She had believed he had shown her the heights of pleasure, but that . . . that had been so powerful, and so strangely primitive, it had been like . . . mating. Like two wild creatures meeting in a fiery joining for reasons they couldn't comprehend.

She didn't think she'd be able to look him in the eye. Surely it would be visible, marking her somehow, like a brand. Something so primitive *had* to leave a sign of change, because she was different from yesterday. Yesterday, she had known she belonged to him.

Today, he knew it.

She couldn't hide from him now. Sometime during the starkly primitive joining, she had lost that ability. He had made her his so utterly that it was no longer her secret.

Erin raised her head cautiously, and felt her heart turn over when she looked at his face. He was deeply asleep, and she'd never seen him like that. It was as close as he'd come to being completely vulnerable, she thought, his strong features relaxed, enigmatic violet eyes hidden. And she loved him so much—

Had she told him that? Or was that part of the dream? Not that it mattered. If he didn't know, he would the moment he looked at her.

Carefully, she eased away from him, almost holding her breath when he made a rough sound that, even in sleep, was a little impatient. A slight frown pulled at his brows, but then smoothed away, and he didn't wake. Erin slid from the bed, making sure he was still covered up, then got her robe from the floor—it had been on the bed last night—and put it on.

Half an hour later, having left a note for him on the nightstand, she was running on the beach, trying to understand how it was possible to feel so happy and yet so scared. She hadn't found an answer for that by the time she finished her run, or when she changed into her swimsuit in one of the cabanas and claimed a lounge chair by the pool.

She swam a few laps lazily, more to cool off from her run than anything else, then climbed out and made herself comfortable in her chair. An attentive poolside waiter placed a small table beside her and went off to fetch coffee and fruit, and after she'd politely but firmly rebuffed three tanned strangers in the space of a few minutes, she was left alone to enjoy her breakfast.

People had been smiling at her all morning, and that was unusual; it was an instant, almost instinctive smile, the way people smiled at the innocent emotions of babies and young lovers. She thought her happiness was showing, that everyone saw, not just Keith, and uneasily put on sunglasses because she felt like a neon sign. It wasn't that she was ashamed of her feelings, it was just that it was an unnervingly naked sensation. She was accustomed to people noticing how she looked, but not how she felt.

And what about Keith? How would he react? Last night, after talking to her father, Erin had decided that while she could accept, sadly, the distance between her and her father, she was determined to bridge the space Keith had set between them. The worry was how to accomplish that. She had fallen asleep still trying to come up with an answer.

She loved him—and today he would know that. Would it make a difference to him? Could her love, freely offered whether or not he wanted it, ease the violent conflicts she sensed in him—or only make his struggle worse? How could she find the source of his trapped rage and release it? And would he even give her the time to try once he knew?

Questions. And no answers.

"Excuse me?"

The voice was a deep, gentle baritone, and she looked up prepared to politely refuse another offer of companionship from a stranger. But when she looked at this stranger, the automatic rebuff died in her throat.

He was a very big man with a curious aura of strength despite old age, upright and powerful though one of his elegant hands rested on a gold-headed cane. He was dressed all in white, his suit starkly formal in the casual setting, and both his thick hair and full beard were snowy, almost radiant. Dark, smiling eyes looked down at her with an oddly vivid wisdom, and his smile was . . . something special.

"I don't mean to intrude," he said softly. "If you'd rather, I can go away again."

Forever afterward, Erin was unable to explain the instant fascination she felt, the warm and certain trust. She had the most peculiar impulse to say: *Where have you been, I've been waiting for you!* And she had no idea why. It was almost dreamlike. She found herself gesturing toward a nearby cushioned, rattan chair, watching him pull it closer and sit down, looking into his face with wonder and pleasure.

"Most people don't recognize me," he said in that amazingly kind, tranquil voice. "But you do, I think."

"I—I feel I do. I can't explain it."

"There's no need. My name is Fortune, if that helps."

She tilted her head a little as she looked at him, reaching up almost unconsciously to remove her sunglasses so there'd be no barrier between them. "Fortune . . . Yes, of course. I've seen you before. Long ago, when I was a child."

He nodded, smiling.

"I was lost," she remembered slowly. "I'd gone riding in the mountains, and my horse threw me. It was very cold, and I'd forgotten the way back. I was afraid. And then you were just there. You took my hand and walked with me for hours until we reached the lodge. I looked for you later, but you weren't there, and nobody seemed to know you." She paused, then added softly, "A blizzard came that night."

"Our lives have crossroads," he said, answering a question she couldn't put into words. "Sometimes all we need is a guiding hand to turn us in the right direction. You were meant to be here. I had to make sure you were."

Without hesitation, she said, "That's why you're here now."

"Yes, child."

"To help me."

"To help you both."

Erin half nodded, accepting. "He's so angry," she said. "I don't know how to touch him there. I think I'm afraid to touch him there."

"You must, child. You're the only one who can."

"Because I love him?"

"Yes. He needs your love."

She didn't find it at all strange to be talking this way to this man, and she wasn't even aware of the trust in her voice. "But how can I, when he won't let me?"

Gently, Fortune said, "When grief and rage fill the emptiness in a man's heart, it's a terrible thing. If he holds it inside, it feeds on itself and grows stronger until it becomes the master. Then he walks in a dark place, too far from the light to see he's lost his way."

"What can I do?"

"Love him."

"He doesn't want my love."

"Are you so sure? The love of a woman is a precious thing; few men throw it away carelessly. Child, in all matters of love, there comes a point when you must trust in the strength of what you feel. And to every man comes a moment when he must decide what it is he wants most of all. When that time comes, you'll know."

Erin understood what he was saying, and it frightened her. "What if he turns away from me?" she whispered. "What if his anger is stronger than I am?"

"Courage, child." He reached out one elegant hand to fleetingly touch her cheek, and then rose to his feet. "The bond between you is strong, and rooted more deeply than his anger. Hold on to it. Trust your love for him."

She looked away from Fortune for the first time, gazing blindly at the sparkling blue water of the pool. When she looked back, he was gone.

She didn't question the strange meeting. In- stead, she reached into the totebag beside her chair and drew out her sketchpad. It was half filled with sketches now, most of which she had done last night after Keith had gone, and she turned the pages steadily until she reached a blank one. She drew for a long time, and when she was finished she tore out one of the two sketches she had just completed. She put it face-down on the chair where Fortune had sat, then took one of the fresh flowers from the vase on her breakfast tray and placed it on top of the sketch. Then she put the pad away.

She rearranged her lounge chair and stretched out on her stomach, letting the sun's heat seep into her muscles. She would have sworn she didn't fall asleep, but the next time she glanced over at the chair, her offering was gone.

It was after ten when Erin heard footsteps crossing the tile toward her, and for the first time that morning she was alone at the pool. She was sitting up again, wearing her sunglasses as she gazed meditatively toward the ocean, and though her pulse speeded up she was able to respond to Keith's rather abrupt greeting calmly.

"How long have you been out here? You'll burn," Keith said, sitting down in the chair beside her.

"I never burn. Another result of good genes, I suppose. Besides, I'm wearing sunblock."

"That's about all you're wearing."

Erin looked down at her—quite modest—one-piece green swimsuit, then turned her gaze to Keith. Through her sunglasses, he looked brooding. If she hadn't dreamed those words of love, and he had heard them, either he didn't remember or else had no intention of bringing up the subject. She was suddenly terrified to let him see, terrified that he would take one look and walk away from what he didn't want.

"Have you eaten?" she asked, ignoring the remark about her swimsuit.

"No." He reached over and removed her sunglasses.

She immediately looked away, saying, "You should. We could have an early lunch, or—"

"Erin."

That flat voice she knew so well. But she was afraid to look at him without the shield of the glasses, because she knew her heart would be in her eyes, she could still feel the sensation of naked neon emotion beaming from her. Anything would be better than losing him. Anything.

Hurriedly, she said, "I think you're right. I've been out here long enough." She slid from the lounge, away from him, and stood to put on the wraparound skirt that went with her suit, and step into her sandals. Before she could reach for her tote, he was there, standing squarely in front of her, his hands reaching out to hold her bare, sunwarmed shoulders with a force that stopped just short of pain.

"Erin, did I hurt you?" His voice was low now, a little rough. "Last night, when I came back, did I hurt you?"

She stared at the top button of his casual sportshirt and shook her head. "No. No, of course not."

"Then what's wrong? Why won't you look at me?"

She closed her eyes for a moment, knowing that it was no good, she couldn't lie or evade. "Because I broke the rules. Your rules." Opening her eyes, she looked up at him.

Keith was absolutely motionless for what seemed like eternity, his brilliant gaze locked with hers, and then he yanked her into his arms and held her tight. The hard angle of his jaw rubbed her temple as he muttered huskily, "I thought I was mistaken last night. But you did say it, didn't you?"

"Yes." She slipped her arms around his waist, holding on to him even though she knew all too well that in ten minutes he could still walk away. Right now, he wanted her love, and for right now that was enough. Her face was hidden against his neck, and she could feel a pulse hammering there, feel his heart beating quickly and hard in his chest.

Keith drew back just a little, his hands lifting to surround her face. His expression was taut, his eyes still blazing with an intensity so bright she almost wanted to look away from it.

"Say it again," he ordered in a low voice.

"I love you, Keith." She said it simply, her voice gentle and eyes steady. "I have from the beginning. Even before we really met, I think."

He made a rough sound that was almost an oath, angry, but he was kissing her and there was hunger in his kiss, and possessiveness, and a satisfaction that was fiercely male. Erin hadn't expected tender words from him, but she felt a pang anyway, because it was a bittersweet feeling to offer her love and have it accepted so ambivalently. It didn't help much to know he was torn, that a powerful conflict raged inside him; no woman wanted to know her love caused pain, that it hurt instead of healed.

But she said nothing, because he'd granted her no right by accepting her love. There was still a wall between them, and she wasn't yet ready to pit her own strength against it.

Without another word, Keith released her and gathered up her things, then took her hand firmly and led her into the hotel. She knew what he wanted, what they both wanted; their passion was so strong and uncomplicated that it swept everything else aside, leaving no room for anything except the pleasure they found in each other's arms. And because that was all he would give her now, because she was bound by her love to give him all that she was, she held nothing back.

That morning set the tone for the next two days. Having accepted her love, Keith was different only in that he didn't say another word about their relationship; he didn't question, didn't insist he was bad for her, and was far less contradictory than he'd been before. His desire for her seemed to grow more intense, and her response deepened until even a glance from him was enough to kindle a fire inside her.

He left each evening, literally tearing himself away from her, and returned in the dark predawn hours so tightly wound with strain it was like an aura around him. There was something hard-edged about him when he first returned, something almost violent and dangerous. He was rougher then, his need unhidden, his desire potent. She couldn't help but respond to that, her body like a hair trigger to his touch. It never frightened her, but what she felt in him made her anxiety grow.

The most difficult thing she'd ever done in her life was to ask him no questions. She couldn't hold back her own words of love, not once he knew, but clung grimly to at least the spirit of the terms she'd agreed to. In her father's world, with all its subtlety and deception, an agreement had to be honored, a promise upheld; over the years she had gained a deep understanding of how important it was to stand by one's word.

At first, it helped to know that she was good for Keith. The passion between them seemed to . . . anchor him somehow, help him to regain his balance when he returned in the night so tormented by his demons. He slept deeply afterward, waking late in the morning, and for a few hours he'd be almost relaxed, able to laugh at her bemusement when she demanded to know how on earth they'd wound up on the floor, or when she told him some of the comical stories of growing up in the diplomatic corps.

"You did *what?*"

"Well, the American ambassador's daughter told me that all sheikhs went berserk over redheads, and I knew his fourth wife was only a year older than I was, so when he gave Dad a camel, I was convinced he was trying to buy me. I was so terrified that I hid, and somehow or other I got locked into the women's quarters, and Mother thought I'd been kidnapped. . . ."

He watched her constantly, and at first she thought the anger in him was lessening. But, gradually, she realized that it was stronger than ever—only more deeply contained. It dawned on her finally that there was a tug of war going on.

By the third morning, she knew. She knew what this was costing him. He had returned later than usual last night, finding her awake on the balcony, and he'd been wearing a tuxedo that bore the faint scents of smoke and exotic perfume. He had held her as if she were his lifeline, with a desperation that had moved her unbearably, and even as she had responded wildly to his desire, she had recognized the moment Fortune had foretold.

It was after ten when she heard Keith's shower running. She was in the sitting room of his suite, dressed more decorously than usual in slacks and a sedate blouse. She had ordered brunch an hour before, but hadn't been able to touch anything except coffee. She was on her third cup when he came out of his bedroom in jeans, his thick hair still damp from the shower.

He came toward her, smiling, but the smile died and his eyes narrowed as he stopped suddenly a couple of feet from her position at one end of the couch. "What's wrong?"

"Am I so easy to read?"

"Yes."

She was hardly surprised; the question had been a somewhat ironically rhetorical one. But she managed to keep her voice quiet and almost tranquil, leaning heavily on all the years of being a diplomat's daughter and an asset to his career.

"The coffee's still hot," she said.

Barely taking his eyes off her, Keith went over to the table by the balcony doors and poured a cup for himself. Watching him, she wondered with a pang if he realized that there were new threads of silver in his hair and a finely drawn exhaustion in the tautness of his face. His will was relentless, his strength almost indomitable, but there was a limit beyond which even the strongest of men would be destroyed; she wondered if he even knew how close to the edge he really was.

"What's wrong, Erin?"

She couldn't put it off any longer, couldn't deceive herself into hoping it wasn't necessary. Steadily, she said, "I can't stay with you, Keith. I have to go."

He set his cup back on the table with unnatural

care, and his eyes went curiously blank. "What are you talking about?"

It was almost impossible for her to hold on to control when he asked that harsh question, but she managed to. Barely. "Maybe you can't see what it's doing to you. Maybe you don't want to see. But I do. And I can't be a part of it anymore."

"Erin—"

"It's destroying you. You go out at night, and whatever you're doing is eating you up inside, and then you come back to me but only halfway. I've felt it all along, but now I can see it, and it scares the hell out of me."

He moved slightly, jerkily, as if he would have crossed the space between them, but then went still. "Are you afraid of me?" he demanded in a stony voice.

"No. I never was, even in the beginning. But I'm afraid *for* you. Whatever you're doing is wrong, and it's killing you."

"It isn't wrong. You don't know what you're talking about. I told you—"

"Yes, you told me you weren't a criminal, what you're doing here isn't illegal. It probably isn't. There are some things the law just doesn't cover. But it doesn't make them right. I know you're obsessed, and angry, and have been for a long time. But I promised not to ask questions, so I'm not asking, Keith. I'm just telling you I can't be part of it anymore."

"You aren't part of it." His voice was edging away from control now, tensing with anger. "I made sure."

"By holding me away? Do you even realize what that made me? One side of a tug of war. You want me, but your obsession, your blind anger, keeps pulling you away. I don't know what it is, or where it comes from, but I know you won't let go of it. I know I can't stay here and watch you be torn apart."

"I can handle it," he said harshly.

Erin looked away from him for the first time, her gaze dropping to her tightly laced fingers. "I can't."

"You can't leave. You love me."

After a moment, she raised her eyes to meet his again, hurting so much she knew he saw it. "That's why I have to leave. I'm sorry, Keith. I'm sorry your obsession matters more to you than love."

It was his turn to look away, and he turned stiffly to stare out the open balcony door. He was so tense that his powerful shoulders were rigid, and when he began speaking abruptly his voice was taut with strain. He talked methodically, but as if some dam had burst despite all his efforts, as if every word was wrenched from him totally against his will.

"My natural father died before I was born; he was an air force pilot, killed flying an experimental jet. I was a year old when my mother married Patrick Calloway. He raised me; I've always thought of him as my real father."

Erin listened silently, her own body tense, sensing the root of his anger had to be exposed this way, slowly, a gradual uncovering of all the layers he had wrapped it in.

"He insisted I keep the name I was born with, and explained it to me carefully when I was a kid and hurt that he wouldn't adopt me. He said that my blood father had been cheated in never knowing me, and that all he'd been able to give me was his name; I had to honor him by keeping it. Dad—Patrick—had everything else, everything I would have given my father if he lived. And he treated me as if I'd been born to him."

"He sounds wonderful," Erin said softly.

"He was. So was my mother. I had a great childhood, filled with love and understanding. I was in high school when my sister was born, and I adored her from the first moment I set eyes on her. She was beautiful, I told you that, and she could wrap anyone around her little finger. She was a good kid, right from the first, not at all spoiled or willful. She would have grown into an incredible woman."

Erin was beginning to feel very cold, and only just stopped herself from crying out, *Not all of them?* But she forced herself to remain still and silent, watching his broad back that was so tense, feeling even across the distance between them the brutal rage clawing at him. She forced herself to wait, and after a moment he went on.

"After college, I began working in Dad's company; from the ground up, we both wanted it that way. It's an engineering firm, based in New York, with offices on the West Coast and in Europe. After a few years, I took over the traveling for Dad, so he and Mom could enjoy more time together. I wasn't home a lot, and I didn't really know what was going on in their lives."

Keith's voice had been growing steadily more remote, quieter and without force or emotion, as if now he were saying words that meant nothing to him. That chilled Erin, because it told her all the turbulent feelings were still trapped in him, and he still wasn't willing or able to release them.

"A little over a year ago," he went on, "I was in Paris, and had been for a few months. The call woke me in the middle of the night. It was a friend of mine, a cop with the NYPD, and he said there'd been an accident. Dad's car had gone off a slippery road in the Catskills. Mom had been with him, and Cathy. They were all dead."

"Keith . . . Oh, Keith, I'm so sorry." She wanted to go to him, comfort him somehow, but she could feel the distance between them was greater than it had ever been, as if he'd withdrawn completely inside himself. And he seemed not even to hear her voice, going on in that dispassionate tone as if he felt nothing.

"All I knew until I got home was that they were dead. And there was so much to do, so many things to take care of. At first I didn't realize there'd been more to it than I'd been told. But I found out. I found out the police were certain it hadn't been an accident, even though they couldn't prove who was responsible. They knew the car had been run off the road deliberately. They even knew who had ordered it done.

"Dad had been involving himself in conservation efforts, something I hadn't known. There was a wealthy businessman with political influence named Guy Wellman, who wanted to acquire a piece of property the conservationists were trying to save. Wellman would have netted millions from the deal; he already had an agreement under the table to sell the property to a foreign conglomerate. Dad was spearheading the fight against him, and it looked like he was winning."

Erin fought to keep her voice steady. "Then it was Wellman who—"

"That lily-white coward?" The total lack of emotion in Keith's voice was almost eerie. "He wouldn't dirty his elegant hands with such a distasteful thing as murder. But he didn't mind crawling in bed with the devil to get it done. He asked a favor of Vincent Arturo, an up-and-coming crime boss with a lot of ambition. Arturo had been scratching for political ties, needing the influence to smooth his climb to the top, and Wellman looked like the perfect tool.

"So Wellman went to Arturo. Arturo's old-line mafia, and they know how to protect themselves. He set up the hit in such a way that no one would ever be able to prove he gave the order, even if the police found the men who'd actually run the car off the road.

"When Dad was killed, the conservationist group he'd been working with yelled murder. That was the first I'd heard of it. But over the next few months, I found out the rest. Pieced it together, just like the police had. All the circumstantial evidence that would never reach the inside of a courtroom. Until I was sure."

Keith turned suddenly to face her, his face like granite and eyes completely shuttered. His voice was still remote and dispassionate when he said, "Then I came here to destroy them."

Eight

"How?" Erin whispered. He was so far away from her now that he looked at her as if from the cold, dark reaches of some alien place with no way to get back and no will even to try.

"By playing on their greed and mistrust," Keith explained in that distant voice. "Wellman came down here because he'd found out too late what it meant to have Arturo's claws in him and he wanted to get away. Arturo followed, because he'd had his eye on the drug traffic in Florida and thought he could control this territory—if he could find a way to remove Martine, the man who was already in charge here. The setup was perfect. Wellman was squirming, Arturo was demanding more and more of him—more introductions, more influence, more of his flesh than just a pound. Arturo didn't have the manpower to declare war on Martine, but he was working to get it. They hated and mistrusted each other."

Erin swallowed hard. "What did you do?"

Keith took a step away from the doors and sat down in a chair near the table. His gaze was fixed on her unwaveringly. "I created a Colombian drug cartel, and made myself their representative. It was absurdly easy. All I needed was enough money, and I had that. A faked identity, a boat and jet with Colombian registry, a few paper holding companies with impressive cash balances, a bribe or a favor here and there so that anyone checking would find what I wanted them to. It took a few months to set up, and then all I had to do was come here, splash money around, and meet the right people."

"Wellman. And Arturo."

He nodded slowly. "For nearly three weeks, I've been setting them up. Wellman thinks my cartel will get Arturo off his back because we intend to kill him and deal with Martine; all I ask of Wellman is a little political clout in return. The same deal he made with Arturo, in fact. Poetic justice. Arturo believes he's found the backing to launch a war against Martine, that my cartel prefers to see him in charge, so he's gathering his forces. But of course, there is no cartel. Keith . . ."

He didn't seem to hear her. "Arturo can't possibly win a war with Martine, not alone. And Martine is not a forgiving man. Neither is Arturo. You see, I've taped several conversations with Wellman. Damning conversations, all about how my cartel is going to kill Arturo and deal with Martine. Arturo won't like hearing those tapes, and he will. At the proper time, after I've vanished, he'll go after Wellman. And then Martine will go after him."

Erin understood now. She understood it all. *When grief and rage filled the emptiness in a man's heart . . . obsession was born.* Betrayed by a hamstrung legal system, grief and bitterness became a terrible, vengeful rage that had to be satisfied. No, what he was doing was not illegal. There were people who would question if it was even wrong. Erin wasn't sure herself. But she knew one thing: Somewhere in the deepest part of his conscience, Keith knew it wasn't right.

But she didn't know how or even if she could touch that part of him. And she had to try, because if he went through with his plan, he would be left in the end with only an empty shell. She would love a man who no longer existed, a man whose hollow triumph had destroyed him.

"When will it be—the proper time?"

"Tomorrow, I think," he said remotely.

"They'll be killed," she said, feeling desperately unequal to this and so terrifyingly conscious of the vast distance he had put between them.

"Yes."

Her eyes were burning, and she wished she could cry. "Keith, it's wrong. You know it's wrong, or it wouldn't be tearing you up this way."

"They destroyed my family. Without an ounce of compunction, they violently killed three wonderful people. Good people. They have to pay for that."

"It isn't your place to make them pay—"

"Then whose place is it? Nobody else gives a damn, Erin, I found that out. And I won't be able to live with myself until Wellman and Arturo are burning in hell."

"You'll be there too," she said very quietly. "In a living hell. Suffering with them, and because of them. Another victim to add to their lists. Another person destroyed by them."

"No."

"Yes. And why, Keith? What good will it do? It won't bring back the people you love or help them to rest easier. It won't fill the empty places inside you. It won't even give you what you think you want, because it won't be justice! It will be revenge."

"I'll have no blood on my hands."

"No, only on your soul. Like Wellman."

He jerked at that, as if a blow had struck home, but his face remained stony. "I have to do this," he said flatly.

Erin felt as if every breath she drew hurt unbearably. She couldn't reach him. She had tried, had offered every argument she knew, and it hadn't been enough.

. . . he must decide what it is he wants most of all.

Keith had made his decision. There was nothing she could offer that meant more to him than revenge. And she couldn't stay, knowing that. It was breaking her heart.

"I don't have to watch," she said dully, rising slowly to her feet.

He got up as well, but quickly, then went still again, almost frozen, staring at her. "Where are you going?"

"To pack. My flight leaves in the morning. I—don't think I could face Dad just now, so I'll spend a week or so in New England with Mother's family."

"Don't go," he said.

For an instant, Erin thought she heard some emotion in his deep voice now, but her own feelings were so chaotic she decided it was wishful thinking. He looked the same, shut in himself far away from her. She turned and walked steadily to the connecting doors.

"Good-bye, Keith."

He watched her slender figure vanish through the doorway, saw his side close firmly and, a moment later, heard the muted click of her door shutting. He was alone.

It hadn't occurred to him that she would leave, not during the past few days after he knew she loved him. And when she had said it so quietly, said she was leaving him, it had hit him like a punch to the gut, almost paralyzing him. He had felt numb, dazed. He'd even said it, said she couldn't go because she loved him, as if it were a talisman to ward off the unthinkable.

He had told her all of it, answering the questions she hadn't asked, thinking when she understood, maybe she wouldn't go. She had understood, and she hadn't been horrified as he had once feared she might be, but the most dreadful pain had shadowed her haunting eyes.

And she had left him.

Her gentle voice kept echoing in his head, saying things he had brushed aside, things that wouldn't leave him alone now, beating against his certainty. That he was destroying himself, that it was revenge he wanted, that he'd have blood on his soul like Wellman. That she was leaving. That she couldn't be a part of it anymore, she was leaving. That she couldn't watch what was happening to him, she was leaving.

Maybe you can't see what it's doing to you. Maybe you don't want to see. But I do.

Gone.

You go out at night, and whatever you're doing is eating you up inside, and then you come back to me but only halfway.

Her sweet voice, gone.

But I'm afraid for you. Whatever you're doing is wrong, and it's killing you.

Her fiery passion, gone.

Do you know what that made me? One side

of a tug of war. You want me, but your obsession, your blind anger, keeps pulling you away.

Her love, gone.

I can't stay here and watch you be torn apart . . . I'm sorry your obsession matters more to you than love.

It was final, he knew. Terribly final. She wouldn't walk back through the door. She had left, not because she didn't love him, but because she did.

Stiffly, he began pacing the room, the pressure inside him building like something alive, clawing desperately to get out. He was trying to think, to sort out what he was feeling, but he could only think about her being gone. Bleak and terrifying coldness seemed to consume everything else inside him. Like a wild animal trapped too long in its cage, he paced, knowing there was a door, escape, but wary of trying for freedom—and failing.

His anger had been with him so long, driving him, tormenting him until he'd had to take action, until anything had seemed better than living with it. Until the thought of destroying the two men who had stolen the people he loved had taken root in the anger, feeding on it savagely.

No . . . not blood on my hands or my soul, she was right, I can't live with that.

Was she right about the rest too? Instead of healing the raw wound of his grief and fury, had all the months of obsessive planning, all the tensions and strain, done nothing except more damage? Grief to bitterness, bitterness to rage, rage to hate and revenge, until—what? Until he was an emotional cripple, unable to feel anything?

But he did feel now, he could still feel something other than hate, he told himself.

He felt about Erin. So crucially important to him, connected to some deep part of him in a way he hadn't tried to understand. Offering her love, and he'd wanted it, he'd accepted it, yet held it out away from him because he couldn't pull her over the edge with him.

The realization was like a blow. He had never really believed Erin might be threatened by his plot, not seriously; he'd been too careful to protect his real identity. She had never been in danger from it. She had been in danger from him. He had known all along he wasn't coming back. Whether his revenge ended in success or in failure, he could never go back to being the man he had been. And he hadn't wanted to destroy Erin as well as himself.

Because he loved her.

Keith blinked, looking around him with the dazed eyes of a man who had been in the dark for a long time. Hours had passed, he thought; the balcony was shadowed and the room was dim. He was standing in the middle of the room as if he were lost. But he wasn't, not now. Not any longer. The connection to Erin, something he understood now and didn't struggle against, was pulling him surely in the single direction that mattered, away from the grinding pressure, the blind rage. Not toward emptiness, but toward the love in her eyes, the sweetness of her smile, the pure white flame of her passion.

Love did matter more to him than revenge.

He went quickly to the connecting doors, opening his side quietly. Hers was firmly shut, but when he pushed, it opened without protest. He stepped into her suite and closed the door silently behind him. He could see into her bedroom from here, see a closed suitcase on the floor by the bed and another open on a luggage rack.

She was in the sitting room, in a chair near the

couch, lamplight touching her bright hair with muted fire. Her head was bowed, her face hidden by her hands, and the mute anguish in every line of her body went through Keith like a knife.

"Erin," he said huskily.

She shuddered. "Don't. Please, don't. I can't take anymore." Her voice was thready.

He crossed the space between them swiftly, dropping to his knees beside her chair and grasping her delicate wrists gently. "Erin, honey, look at me." He tried to pull her hands away from her face without force. "Please, baby, look at me."

She did, finally, her huge green eyes wet and deeply shadowed, and the look of blind suffering nearly killed him. He groaned and surrounded her face with his hands, leaning over to kiss her tenderly, muttering words that were quick and urgent with the overwhelming need to ease her pain.

"Oh, dear God. . . . Oh, Erin, I'm sorry, I never wanted to hurt you. I love you, sweetheart, I love you so much. Don't say it's too late, I couldn't bear it if I lost you too."

Erin had been caught in the storm of his emotions more than once, but this time it was almost too much for her. The leap from defeat and misery to hope was so sudden, she was terrified none of this was real, terrified she was dreaming the husky tenderness of his voice, the words of love, and the heart-stopping expression in his vivid eyes.

"You love me?" she whispered.

He groaned again and yanked her against him, his arms going around her hard. He was still on his knees beside her chair, still wearing nothing but jeans, and the heat of his bare skin seemed to burn through her blouse and ease the chill of her own flesh.

"God, yes, I love you," he said thickly, his fingers stroking her hair, her back, almost compulsively. "Don't go, baby, stay with me."

The possibility of his love was something she had wanted so desperately that everything in her cried out now to give in to him, to hold on fiercely to their love and believe that it could pull him free of the anger she could still feel. But she had seen the root of his obsession, and she didn't think she was strong enough to fight it.

"I can't stay," she said almost wildly, clinging to him despite her words. "It would kill me to see you destroyed, don't you understand that? Don't make me watch, Keith, please!"

He uttered a rough sound and scooped her up into his arms with that astonishing strength of his, rising from his knees to sit in her chair and cradle her on his lap. "No, sweetheart, it's all right. It won't happen, I promise. I don't care about that anymore, it doesn't matter. As long as you stay with me, nothing else matters."

She lifted her face from his neck, afraid to believe, but the unshuttered truth in his eyes convinced her. The anger was still pulling at him, she could feel that; it was still inside him because he hadn't dealt with the grief and bitterness that had caused it. But he would, when he was ready. For now, he had turned his back on revenge and reached out to love.

"I love you," he said deeply, stroking her cheek with his fingers in a tender touch. "I've loved you all along, Erin. I was too blind to see it, too obsessed to let myself understand what I was feeling."

Her arms went around his neck, and Erin cuddled closer, the coldness inside her finally vanishing and happiness growing. "I was so afraid. I didn't want to leave you, but I just couldn't stand it anymore. You wouldn't let me get close, and I love you so much I couldn't bear to watch you going further and further away from me."

His arms tightened around her. "That's what made me realize. When you walked through the door and I knew you weren't coming back. I'd convinced myself I could have you and still do what I'd planned, but all the time . . . How could I plot to destroy life, anyone's life, and then look into your eyes? You were so sweet and loving, so gentle. Every time I came back to you, it was like I was bringing the dirt with me, touching you with it, and I hated that. So I kept trying to push you away, even though I couldn't let go of you."

Erin drew back just enough to look into his face, her own delicate features grave. "What are you going to do now?"

"I'll stop it," he said instantly. "The man I pretended to be—Duncan—will vanish from the face of the earth. I made the arrangements to do it in the beginning. It'll only take a phone call to put everything in motion. I won't have to go near them or any of it again. The boat and jet will disappear, the bank accounts will empty, the holding companies turn out to be nothing but paper."

"What will happen?"

He smiled crookedly. "Arturo will scream at Wellman for introducing him to a phantom, and probably bolt for the Northeast out of Martine's territory. Wellman will probably stay here and wonder what the hell happened."

"Are you sure?"

"Pretty sure. Neither of them knows I told a different story to the other. Once I disappear from their lives, all they can have are a lot of questions and no answers. I hadn't pushed them over the edge yet, and now I never will."

"Can you let go of it?" Erin asked hesitantly. "Really let go, I mean? If you're walking away only because *I* couldn't take it, you'll never be free, Keith."

He shook his head slightly, his eyes steady. "I can let go. I have. When all this started, I'd lost everything. I didn't have anything else to hold on to, no way to fight the anger. Now I have you. I'm looking at life instead of death, feeling love instead of hate. I don't want revenge anymore, Erin. I don't need it. All I need is you."

"I love you," she murmured.

She was radiant with happiness, her haunting eyes glowing with love, her beautiful face softened and tender, and he could hardly believe the incredible luck that had brought her to him. And then he had come so close to throwing it all away. . . . He'd been such a blind fool, a real bastard more than once, and yet Erin loved him. He didn't deserve her love, but he knew he would spend the rest of his life trying.

"I love you, too, baby," he said huskily, kissing her with all the gentleness a man of his unruly temperament could claim. Still, after an intensely emotional day, it was hardly surprising that the desire between them would have been heightened, particularly by acknowledgments of love.

It was burning now. Keith became suddenly, achingly conscious of the warm weight of her in his lap, the firm pressure of her breasts against his chest, the bold yet somehow delicate response of her tongue to his. He kissed her again and again, claiming her now, his love feeding a desire too hungry to ever be satisfied. He'd come so close to losing her that now he wanted to love her wildly, to give her all he'd held back before, all of himself.

Drawing back just far enough to take a ragged breath, he looked at the huge green eyes that were sleepy with desire, the soft lips reddened and moist from his kisses. She was lying against him limply, warm and more than willing, everything he wanted and needed, and only his love was strong enough to hold desire at bay for a moment so he could admit something that had been bothering him.

"I've been such a bastard," he muttered, kissing her once more because he had to. "Telling you it was sex or nothing, keeping you in this hotel—hell, mostly the bedroom—as if that was all that mattered to me. Feeling crazy with jealousy if you went out to the beach or pool without me, or even if you smiled at the room service waiter."

"Did you?" Her mouth curved slowly. "Except for the remark about by bathing suit, I didn't see any sign of jealousy."

His laugh was low and a little rough. "Did you notice a couple of days ago when we started being served by a female waiter?"

Erin blinked, then said, "You didn't—?"

"Damned right I did. I knew I was going to take that boy's head off if I caught him smiling at you once more—even if it *was* the most anxious-to-please puppy dog smile I've ever seen on a human face. So I called the manager." Keith felt a sheepish grin tugging at his lips. "I told him there was nothing wrong with the kid's service. I just had this uncontrollable urge to deck any male past puberty who came within ten feet of my lady. I guess hotel managers get used to wild requests;

he said there was no problem at all, he'd just assign us a female waiter, as polite as can be. And he did."

"I can't believe you did that," she said wonderingly.

"I wanted you all to myself. But it wasn't fair to you, Erin. Do you realize that except for a couple of walks on the beach, we haven't left this hotel together since we met? We've barely left the suites. You must have thought I didn't want anything except a sexual toy."

"You as good as told me that." She lifted one eyebrow at him, ruefully amused.

"I was an arrogant bastard, and I'm sorry."

"I can't say I didn't mind, at least in the beginning when you were stating your 'terms' so brusquely. My pride had already gone down without a whimper, and once I realized I loved you, I had to take whatever you were willing to give me. It hurt, but not as much as it might have."

Keith winced. "If it's any comfort, I barely knew what I was saying or doing. I had some damned stupid idea that everything would be fine if I could just get you into my bed."

Erin couldn't help it; she giggled. It was the tone of his voice, so sheepish.

"I swear, Erin, I wasn't thinking at all. I thought a hell of a lot before we became lovers, even if most of what I thought didn't make sense, but after that it was totally useless. All you had to do was smile at me, and I couldn't string three words together without tripping over two of them."

She wondered suddenly if that was why his lovemaking had always been virtually silent, but didn't ask. She was too busy feeling both surprise at his words and a deep contentment at the confirmation of what she'd first believed about him:

His emotions would always be honest ones, and now that he wasn't holding her away, he didn't hesitate to reveal them.

"You never seemed to realize what you did to me," he said, his arms tightening around her. "I couldn't stop looking at you, touching you; if it had been more than three hours since I'd last made love to you, I started going wild—heart pounding, hands shaking, with no more control than a teenager. And right from the first you've been so completely natural with me. Warm and sweet, and so giving."

"The first," she murmured, touching his lean face gently. "That really bothered you, didn't it?"

He kissed her a bit fiercely, and admitted, "The possessive part of me loved it; there's something so damned primitive in knowing you were a woman's first lover. But it also shook me up, more than a little—partly because I'd never been a woman's first lover before."

"You hadn't?"

Keith shook his head. "I'd never thought much about it, to be honest. There have been women, but . . ."

"But?" she prompted, feeling a small stab of jealousy of her own, even though those women had passed through his life before she had even known he existed.

"I was never deeply involved with any of them, and I felt casual about my relationships. A little dinner, a little dancing, a little sex."

"Do I really want to hear this?" Erin murmured almost to herself.

He smiled his crooked smile at her. "Sorry. The point is, I never felt casual about you. It was all instinct and tangled emotion. That first night I had to leave you, I nearly went out of my mind the whole time I was gone, terrified that I'd come back and you wouldn't be here. When I saw you curled up in my bed, the relief was staggering. And then I wanted you so desperately I couldn't even wait long enough to wake you up."

"I remember." She kissed his wry mouth, her own tender. "I'd thought it was a dream."

"I know. You were dreaming, and I couldn't stand not being sure that I was the lover in your dream. Lord, Erin, if I'd only been able to think clearly, I would have known I loved you. What I felt was so overwhelming it couldn't have been anything else. I should have seen that."

"As long as you know now, that's all that matters."

"I know I hurt you," he said roughly. "Treating you the way I did. I swear I'll make it up to you somehow."

"Keith, I love you." Her big eyes were grave and gentle. "And even when you didn't know you loved me, you made me feel loved and needed. Just go on loving me, it's all I want."

He groaned softly, bending his head to capture her warm lips. The desire that had stirred earlier woke again, racing through him like fire in his veins. But now, because he loved her and knew it, all the other primitive feelings made sense.

The fire in her, the incredibly explosive and uninhibited passion, rose to meet his instantly, making his thoughts spin into oblivion and his body shudder with need. Still kissing her deeply, he stood with her in his arms and carried her into the bedroom.

Clothes fell where they were carelessly thrown, some landing in the open suitcase she hadn't finished packing. The bedroom was dim with approaching evening, but they could see each other; it was all that mattered. Their hunger was absolute, and they were so attuned to each other it was as if they were two halves of a single life, each half complementing the other to form a perfect whole. Her fire matched his, her sweetness tempered his force, her gentleness assuaged his turbulent nature, and her love spread a healing balm over his wounded soul.

He had taught her passion but, much more than that, it was Keith's vitality that had unlocked a part of Erin she hadn't known existed. The overwhelming intensity of him, the raw, honest emotions he wasn't afraid to let her see had, from the first, allowed her to free her own. With him, she could be herself. With him, there was no demand to be anything except what she was. And it allowed her to be all she could be.

"I love you," she said huskily, staring up into those fierce, wonderful eyes that were no longer enigmatic or shuttered. Now they were clear and vivid, nakedly expressive of everything he was feeling, and he felt so much she was humbled by it.

"I almost lost you," he said tautly. "Oh, Erin, I love you so much!" His hands were shaking as they moved over her slender body, and he kissed her frantically as if to assure himself she was real, she was there.

She gave him the assurance he needed, taking fire in his arms, murmuring her love and hunger as her body responded to his touch. She lost control in his arms, but that was perfect, that was wonderful, because he lost control too. They were connected . . . bonded . . . mated . . . and when the hunger grew too intense, when necessity demanded the completion that was flesh as well as spirit and emotion, it was like nothing they

had ever experienced before, so incredibly powerful that it left them drained of everything except
the certain knowledge that they belonged to each
other.

They spent the remainder of that evening quietly, close together. Saying little except with glances
and touches. When they realized that neither of
them had eaten, they ordered food. When they felt
like sleeping, they did.

Erin woke sometime around dawn to find herself alone in bed. She got up and shrugged into
a robe. She went into the sitting room and saw
that the balcony doors were open. Keith was
there, standing naked as he stared out over the
ocean. Silently, she joined him, sitting down on
the chaise.

"I didn't want to wake you," he murmured.

"It's all right." She looked at him, so vital and
compelling, his muscled body magnificent in the
stark gray light of dawn, so strong and proud.
And, very gently, she repeated, "It's all right,
Keith."

He shuddered, as if shaken by a wave of intolerable emotion, and then began to talk. His voice
was low and hurried, driven from him by the
pressure inside, aching with feeling.

He talked about his family. About the stepfa-
ther who had raised him. About the mother who
had borne him. About the sister who had been
able to wrap him around her finger.

While dawn marked the pause between darkness and light, he talked, sketching the years and
the love, filling in the bare outlines he had offered
her once before. He made his family come alive

for her as they lived in him, made them walk and talk and breathe.

And, finally, as the first bright rays of the morning sun spilled over his powerful frame, he cried. His head buried in her lap, arms wrapped tightly around her. All the corrosive anger and bitterness, and the desolate grief, released at last in acid tears that would begin the healing.

Nine

Almost a week later, as Erin and Keith entered their Nassau hotel after having spent the morning and early afternoon out on the sailboat he had rented, she paused to say, "Hold on a second; I want to buy a newspaper and find out what's going on in the rest of the world." She raised herself on tiptoe to kiss his chin. "I'll be right back."

He stood watching her cross the lobby to the newsstand, admiring the graceful way she moved. She'd put on a denim skirt and blouse over the scandalous swimsuit, an outfit that would have looked casual on any other woman and was stunning on her.

How he loved her! He still considered it the most miraculous thing that she loved him. And probably, he thought, always would. After what he'd put her through. . . . But she did love him, and the vast warmth of that filled all the places inside him that had once held only blind anger.

"Mr. Donovan?"

Something about the emotionless voice touched a faint cord of memory, and he turned his head quickly. The first thing he saw was the discreet flash of a badge, the wallet containing it opened and closed so smoothly that he doubted anyone else in the busy lobby had noticed. The second thing he saw was the hard face and shuttered eyes of Wellman's assistant, and though that was a shock, it was less unpleasant than it might have been because of the badge; the man was a federal cop.

"My name's Masters, Mr. Donovan. I'm with the Justice Department."

Keith stared at him thoughtfully. "How odd. The last time I saw you, you were fetching and carrying for Guy Wellman."

A thin smile touched Master's lips. "You should be glad I was, Mr. Donovan. That fabricated background was good—damned good for an amateur—but there were a couple of loose threads. I snipped them."

With almost idle curiosity, Keith said, "And I suppose you followed me from the boat back to the hotel one night. That was careless of me."

"No, you weren't careless. It was just that I'd been on Wellman for more than a year. I knew who you were."

Keith shook his head a little, still showing no more than faint interest in the subject. "Yeah, I counted too much on being unknown to all the players. Definitely amateur time. Any particular reason you've looked me up now? I mean, am I going to be hauled back to Miami and arrested for impersonating a drug lord?"

"Hardly. I thought you might like to know what's happened since you folded your tent."

"What's happened to whom?"

"Wellman and Arturo, naturally."

The radar that never failed him where she was

concerned alerted Keith, and he turned his head to see Erin coming back across the lobby. Absently, he said, "They can live for all I care."

"Generous of you," Masters said with something of a snap, both surprised and a bit irritated. Then he followed the other man's intent gaze, and his mouth fell open. He'd seen beautiful women before, but the redhead coming toward them was like something out of a dream. And it wasn't just the perfection of her delicate features, her vivid coloring, or the centerfold body. She was . . . radiant. Heads were turning all over the lobby to watch her, smiles breaking out almost unconsciously. Masters could feel one pulling at his own strictly trained mouth.

"Sort of takes your breath away, doesn't she?"

The mild question yanked Masters from his trance, and he looked to see Donovan smiling at him. He wanted to step back away from that smile. In fact, he wanted to back away rather hastily. It wasn't a specifically threatening smile, it just made the hair on the back of his neck quiver.

But he stood his ground, and even managed an ironic tone when he answered, "Sort of, yeah."

The redhead reached them just then, tucking a folded newspaper under one arm and reaching out a hand even as Donovan did, their fingers twining with a look of ineffable belonging, as if a connection had been made. Trained to be observant, Masters caught the gleam of two wedding bands.

Well, no wonder he's lost interest in revenge, Masters thought, knowing very well that Donovan had been single when he'd arrived in Florida.

"Erin, this is Mr. Masters; he's with the Justice Department. Masters—my wife, Erin."

"Justice Department?" She looked up at her husband, a hint of worry momentarily dimming her bright eyes.

"It's all right, he hasn't come here to arrest me," Donovan said. It was obvious from his reassuring smile at his wife that she knew the entire story.

Erin turned a somewhat guarded gaze to Masters. "No?"

"No, ma'am," he affirmed, back in control again. "I'd just like to talk to your husband for a few minutes. In private would be best."

"We can go up to the suite," Keith said, and began leading his wife toward the elevators as if he didn't much care whether Masters followed.

"I'd been trying to get to Arturo through Wellman," Masters began a few minutes later, seated in a chair in their sitting room as he looked at the two of them on the couch. "Wasn't having much luck, not with specifics. And I wasn't delighted when Wellman bolted down to Miami—until Arturo followed him. Things finally started to get interesting. Then you showed up."

"A wild card," Keith murmured.

"I'll say. The only thing I knew for sure was that you were after those two. I didn't know what your plan was. By the time I'd figured it out, you were very neatly playing them against each other, and that game was so dangerous I didn't dare interfere."

"So you waited."

"It seemed best. Wellman was acting friendly with Arturo again, spending more time with him, thanks to you, and I was picking up bits and pieces of the kind of information I'd been working to get. Even with the payoff, though, my superiors weren't at all crazy about your participation. I expect to be read the riot act when I get back to D.C. But I had a feeling you could break the whole thing wide open, one way or another, so I made a judgment call and elected to let you run with your plan. And, to be honest, I wasn't exactly anxious to try and pull you out; I knew enough about you—and your motives—to be fairly sure I didn't have a snowball's chance in hell of stopping you, short of putting a bullet in you."

In a faintly surprised tone, as if the man he had been then was a stranger to him now, Keith said, "I was as close as I ever want to be to insanity."

Masters grunted. "Yeah, but crazy like a fox. By the way, if you ever want a job, look me up."

A genuine smile of amusement gleamed in Keith's eyes. "No, thanks. I'm an engineer and a businessman."

The agent gave him a somewhat ironic look, but said, "If you say so. Anyway, I decided to wait and see what developed. Things were shaping up nicely for a territorial war in Florida, which the DEA and Miami vice considered promising; they hadn't been able to get close to Martine until you started stirring the pot. Everyone on both sides was quietly gearing up for an explosion of one kind or another. And then you—or Duncan, I should say—just up and vanished."

Under Erin's fascinated gaze, the federal agent's rather thin smile became almost beatific, and his emotionless voice deepened with pure pleasure.

"To call Wellman's condition one of panic," he said, "would be to understate the matter. The man quite literally went to pieces."

Surprised, Keith said, "Just because I disappeared?"

"Your timing couldn't have been more perfect. You see, Wellman had decided that he was going to be smarter this time. He wanted somebody to owe him for a change."

"He went to Martine?" Keith guessed.

"Bingo. He was feeding Martine all of Arturo's battle plans, as well as information about your cartel. The way he saw it, and the way you had explained it to him, the cartel would remove Arturo before the war got nasty and then cut a deal with Martine—who would be ever so grateful to his dear friend Wellman for all his help."

"It might have worked," Keith said thoughtfully. "If there'd been a cartel."

"Right, but there wasn't. So you vanished, along with every scrap of proof that you'd even existed. And Wellman is left with several very unsettling realizations. *He* introduced you to Arturo, who had planned to declare war on the strength of your supposed backing. *He* betrayed Arturo thinking he'd never get caught out, which now put him squarely between Arturo and Martine. And *he* didn't have an army to protect him."

"Ouch," Keith murmured.

"Uh-huh. And after that, it was easy. He wanted protection so badly he was willing to spill everything. He was terrified that Arturo was going to come after him, and since Martine could be forgiven for thinking he'd been lied to about the cartel as well, he wasn't likely to offer protection. I flashed my badge at the opportune moment, and Wellman started talking. He had a lot to say too. Since Arturo had felt very sure of him, Wellman knew quite a bit about his operations, and enough details about specific crimes—such as the hit on your family—to put them both away for a long, long time."

Erin, who had been listening silently all this time, looked at Keith and said quietly, "Justice."

He nodded slowly, gazing at her, then turned his attention to Masters and said, "I had planned to push them a lot harder. I was out for blood."

"I know," the agent responded. "Worried me for a while. I'm glad you stopped short of that, though. If you hadn't, it would have been a real mess. This way, they both pay for quite a few past crimes, and you don't have to think of yourself as a vigilante. You pushed them just enough to put them into our hands, and nobody got hurt by it. You were lucky."

"Yes," Keith said, looking at Erin again. "Very lucky."

Masters was a highly trained and keenly observant agent who'd been taught to sense undercurrents, and the one moving between these two was so intense it almost embarrassed him. All his instincts told him it was time to fold his own tent and depart, so he said his good-byes with a minimum of words and left to catch the plane that would take him back to the States.

He couldn't help but think, though, as he left the Bahamas behind, that Keith Donovan had indeed been astonishingly lucky. At a critical point in his life, when an obsession with revenge might well have destroyed him, he had found the only thing capable of pulling him from the blackness of rage and bitterness.

Fate, Masters thought idly, must have had a hand in it.

On a balmy afternoon a few days later, Erin stretched contentedly, as lazy as a cat in the sunshine, her two-piece swimsuit covering only what the law demanded. From her prone position on the deck of the drifting sailboat, she looked drowsily up at the gently swaying mast, allowing its motion and the peaceful ocean to lull her.

"Hey."

She made a faint sound that might have been taken for a response, though it was utterly languid.

"Wake up and talk to me," Keith requested in an aggrieved tone. "Honestly, if I'd known you were part cat and always went to sleep in the sunshine, I never would have rented this boat."

She smiled, closing her eyes. "Can't help it."

A shadow loomed over her suddenly. She opened one mildly distressed eye, then the other, gazing up at him reproachfully. "It felt so good," she explained.

Raised on an elbow beside her, he reached to lay one large hand on her sun-warmed stomach. "So does this."

"Ummm. That's true. All right, I'm awake. What did you want to talk about so badly?"

He smiled down at her, his lean face totally relaxed and peaceful, violet eyes luminous. "I just wanted to hear your voice. Ever since you conked out on me after lunch, I've been lying here listening to seagulls. I've come to the conclusion that your voice is better than the seagulls'."

"Gee, thanks."

He leaned over to kiss her, his lips moving slowly and sensuously on hers, then straightened before she could reach up and grab him. "Oh, no," he said severely with a mock frown.

"Why not?" she murmured, allowing the fingers of one hand to wander across his broad chest. "We're alone out here."

"That's what I thought yesterday," he reminded her. "And if that patrol boat skipper hadn't forgotten his responsibilities, his oath, his country, and his name after one glance at you, we'd probably have been arrested."

Her eyes widened innocently. "I thought he was very nice about it. Especially after you called him a barnacle."

Keith had the grace to look a bit sheepish, but said firmly, "The man was practically drooling."

"Oh, he was not. Just polite and friendly."

"And wonderfully stalwart in his spiffy white uniform," Keith said darkly. "Damn him."

Serenely, Erin said, "I've never cared for men in uniform."

Keith eyed her. "No?"

"No. Had my fill of them at all those embassies."

After considering that for a moment in reflective silence, Keith said, "In that case, I'll stop trying to decide the most satisfying method of separating the hotel's doorman from his most prized body parts."

Erin maintained her tranquil expression. "That would probably be best."

"But it hardly narrows the field," Keith complained, his gloomy voice belied by the amusement in his eyes. "Everywhere I turn, there's some man tripping over his own feet or running into a wall trying to get another look at you."

"Look who's talking," she scoffed. "I happen to know for a *fact* that our room service waiter has been raffling off deliveries so that the other ladies on the staff can get a look at you in a towel—and I hear the price of the tickets is skyrocketing."

"Nonsense."

Erin giggled at his rather startled expression. He really had no idea that the force of his personality combined with the blatant sexuality he exuded drew female eyes wherever he went. As for his possessiveness of her, it was never smothering and didn't disturb her in the slightest, but it was also not—quite—the light matter he made it out to be.

He had explained shortly after their whirlwind marriage with his usual honesty, saying that he'd come so close to losing her he wasn't quite able to get over the fear of it. He doubted he ever would, but promised to try and stop regarding every man between adolescence and death as a threat. In the meantime, Erin concentrated on loving him so much he couldn't possibly feel threatened, and he avoided saying rude things to strangers—the patrol boat skipper had caught him at a vulnerable moment—and teased her about her quite unintentional effect on men.

Erin thought they were both enjoying it.

He eyed her now after her remark about their room service waiter, but apparently decided to let the matter drop. His hand was moving slowly on her sun-warmed stomach, and the building intensity in his gaze made her feel more than the heat of a tropical afternoon.

She slid her arms up around his neck, her fingers threading into his thick hair, and smiled. "I don't think we'll be disturbed today," she murmured. "There isn't a boat anywhere near us."

He might have been able to teasingly resist her a few minutes ago, but Keith had known from the beginning that his hunger for Erin went too deep to be something he could fight. And he didn't want to fight it, not for a long time now. The bond between them had deepened even more these last days, growing stronger and more certain, and their physical response to each other had intensified as well.

Keith lowered his head and kissed her hungrily,

his hands moving with sure knowledge to unfasten the flimsy ties of her brief swimsuit and smooth the material away and then get rid of his own trunks. Her hands were on him as well, soft and strong, exploring the body she knew well now and found more compelling each time she touched it.

The thick pallet of blankets beneath them cushioned them from the sailboat's deck, and the lazy rocking motion of the vessel added an erotic rhythm that was slow and sweet and heated. The sun bore down on them, almost shatteringly bright, and a soft breeze caressed their naked bodies.

Erin thought that it was somehow new each time, the sensations different with every touch. Her body seemed more sensitized, all her senses opening with a completeness she had never even imagined possible, and her love for him filled her heart and mind as if it had always been a part of her.

He was still virtually a silent lover, still unable to say very much in the consuming power of his need for her. The words he did utter were rough and low, love words and sex words that were disjointed, almost wild. He lost control as swiftly and completely as she did, his turbulent nature given over totally to the fierce passion between them. His hands shook as they stroked her body, gentle but somehow primitive, as if all his deepest instincts knew without question that she belonged to him.

And that he belonged to her. He gave himself to her every time they made love, with utter abandon pouring all that he was into the loving. His emotions, so honest and naked, were like a storm, and it was a storm Erin treasured.

It swept over them both, the force in him matched by her, and when it finally passed they were left, drained and content, to bask in a sunlit peace.

She stirred first, just a faint movement that was lazy and blissfully sated. Keith raised himself a bit to make her more comfortable, but remained propped on his forearms as he kissed her smiling lips tenderly. The breeze was cool now on their damp bodies, and a shadow from the lowered sail crept over them as the sun began sinking in the west.

"We should be heading back," he murmured, kissing her again because he had to. He wondered fleetingly if he would ever be able to look at her and not have to touch, to kiss, to lose himself in the magic of her luminous eyes, and thought he knew what the answer was. Never. If fate granted him a dozen lifetimes in which to love her, he might possibly grow accustomed to these incredible feelings, but he knew he would never get over the astonished wonder of knowing she loved him.

"I suppose so." Her voice was soft and dreamy, her green eyes misty with love and contentment as she looked up at him.

He stroked her flushed cheek gently. "Are you sure you don't mind going to New York so soon? I can put them off a few more days."

"I don't mind at all," she said serenely. "Your company's struggled along without you for too long as it is. Besides, it was your idea to have a honeymoon in the Bahamas. I told you I'd be perfectly happy to go straight back to New York, but you wouldn't listen."

"I listened." He kissed her again. "I just felt so guilty. Carrying you off to a judge because I couldn't wait to marry you, barely giving you time to call your father. You didn't have a proper wedding, sweetheart, and I wanted you at least to have a honeymoon."

"My wedding was quite proper, thank you," she told him, smiling. "I don't feel at all deprived. In fact, I've been gloriously happy, in case you haven't noticed. I don't need a lot of pomp and ceremony, darling, only you."

"I love you," he said softly, intensely. "I love you so much."

"I love you too. Isn't it wonderful?"

Keith hugged her, agreeing wordlessly that it was, then reluctantly eased away from her. "If we don't raise the sail and head back right now," he said, "I'm going to get distracted again and we'll never make it."

"You're so reasonable," she said admiringly, her eyes gleaming at him as she found her swimsuit and began putting it on.

Several minutes later, the sails raised and their little boat skimming swiftly over the sparkling water toward Nassau, Keith asked a question that had been troubling him only a little. "Do you think your father's forgiven me yet?"

"Is that bothering you?" she returned politely.

"Not on my account. I married you, not him. I just don't want you to be upset, sweetheart."

She smiled and touched his cheek. "I don't think he'll ever be able to upset me again. We never would have been close, Keith, even if you hadn't come along. And he didn't disown me, you know. In fact, he invited us very civilly to come and spend a few weeks at Westford."

"True. Do you want to?"

"Not particularly. I'd like for you to see the place someday, but there's no hurry."

"Um. Well, in that case, we won't worry about it for a while. I'll probably have to go back to Europe in a couple of months, so we'll visit then."

She grinned a little. "While Dad's in Turkey?"

Keith reached out an arm and drew her close to his side, smiling wryly. "Okay, so I feel a bit wary about meeting a British ambassador whose daughter I eloped with."

"He won't be hostile," Erin said, no longer troubled by the distance between her and her father.

"Maybe not, but I probably will." Keith met her smiling gaze, then shrugged and pushed the matter from his mind. Erin was happy with him, he knew, and that was really all that counted. He meant to make certain that their life together was so complete and filled with love that she wouldn't feel the lack of closeness with her father.

"All I need is you," she said softly, reading his mind or his expression, her eyes glowing as she cuddled close to him.

Keith held her, feeling the brisk wind in his face, the sunlight warm and bright, his heart so full that it seemed it might burst with happiness. And he thought, fleetingly, of the strange old man Erin had told him about, the one who had *known* even though he couldn't have, because it wasn't possible. . . .

But maybe after all, it was quite possible. Maybe destiny supplied a special emissary when a guiding hand was needed, and called him Fortune.

Erin believed that.

Keith thought he did, as well.

Epilogue

"Well, you won again," she said.

"Destiny won, my sweet," he responded, closing a file as he sat at his desk and laying it aside.

Her delicate hand touched his shoulder, and she leaned down to kiss him. "Coming to bed?"

"In a moment," he said, and watched her slender, elegant figure move gracefully from the study.

He sat in a pool of lamplight, his gaze turned inward, a big, powerful, very old man, with a spirit so ageless and filled with delight that it seemed an aura around him. And he thought idly that he hadn't known, back when it all began, how full and rich his life would be. He had been blind, too, then, as stubbornly resistant to the dictates of fate as a fierce young man could be. He hadn't known, hadn't recognized the truth of every soul's search for its match, its mate.

Until his own tempestuous search began.

"I am the captain of my fate," he murmured softly in the peaceful, book-lined room. "I am the master of my soul."

The sound of a low, vastly amused chuckle became a deep and delighted laugh, and upstairs in their bedroom, where she waited for him, Julia heard. And smiled.

THE EDITOR'S CORNER

There's something a little bit forbidden about this month's group of heroes. For one reason or another they seem to be exactly the wrong men for our heroines to fall in love with—but, of course, the six ladies involved do just that, unable as they are to resist the potent allure of these special LOVESWEPT men. And what they feared was forbidden fruit turns out to be necessary to their very existences!

In **TROPICAL HEAT,** LOVESWEPT #432, Patt Bucheister creates a noble hero named John Canada, and she puts his nobility to the test by having him fight his overwhelming passion for Salem Shepherd, the woman he'd first known as a young girl. Together they had escaped from an orphanage and forged a friendship based on trust and need. But the feelings that began to surface in John as Salem blossomed into womanhood scared him, tempted him, thrilled him—and made him realize he had to send her away. Years later Salem returns to help John when his business is in trouble, and the feelings he'd once felt for her pale in comparison to the desire he knows he can no longer fight. These two people who've shared so much find themselves swept away on a current stronger than an ocean surge, right into the arms of destiny. Patt has outdone herself in crafting a love story of immense emotional impact.

Charlotte Hughes gives her heroine something of a dilemma in **RESTLESS NIGHTS,** LOVESWEPT #433. How can Kelly Garrett get on with her life as an independent single mom, when she discovers she's falling for Macon Bridges, a man who represents so much of what she's struggled to put behind her after her first marriage failed. Macon is the successful owner of the firm she works for; he has the tendency to want to take control and do things for her that she's just learned to do for herself; he's dedicated to his job and at times allows it to take top priority in his life. Then again, the man can charm the birds from the trees and certainly knows how to send Kelly's heart into flight! But

(continued)

once this smitten lady makes up her mind to risk it all on the sexy man who's causing her too many restless nights, it's Macon who doesn't stand a chance! Charlotte's lighthearted style makes this story pure entertainment.

TEMPESTUOUS, LOVESWEPT #434, by Tami Hoag, not only describes the feisty heroine in the book, Alexandra Gianni, but also the state of the atmosphere whenever she encounters hero Christian Atherton. The sparks do fly between the aristocratic charmer who is used to having women fall at his feet not throw him to the ground, and the lovely wildcat with the haunted eyes and determined ways of a woman who has something to hide. At first Christian sees winning Alex as a challenge, until he becomes thoroughly enchanted by the spirited woman he yearns to know all about. His wicked reputation seems in jeopardy as he longs only to soothe Alex's sorrow and shower her with tenderness. But not until Alex convinces herself she deserves to be cherished can she accept Christian's gift of love. This poignant romance features several characters from two of Tami's previous books, **RUMOR HAS IT,** #304, and **MAN OF HER DREAMS,** #331, the most notable character of which is hero Christian, whose love story you've asked Tami for in your letters. Enjoy!

Joan Elliott Pickart's **TO LOVE AND TO CHERISH,** LOVESWEPT #435, opens with a dramatic scene that won't fail to grip you. Imagine meeting a stranger in the foggy cocoon of night on a deserted beach. In a moment of yearning desperation, imagine yourself surrendering to him body and soul, then running off without ever learning his name! Heroine Alida Hunter was lost in her grief until she met the man with the summer-sky eyes. But she knew he was a fantasy, a magical gift she could never keep. Paul-Anthony Payton couldn't forget the mysterious woman who'd bewitched him then vanished, and he vowed to find her. She'd filled him with hope that night on the beach, but when he finally does find her, his hopes are dashed by her denial of what they'd shared.

(continued)

Alida's fear of loving and losing terrifies her and prevents her from believing in Paul-Anthony's promises. But the more she tells herself he's the forbidden lover of her dreams, the more Paul-Anthony makes her dreams become reality. Once again Joan delivers a powerful love story LOVESWEPT fans will treasure.

Judy Gill casts another memorable character in the role of hero in **MOONLIGHT MAN,** LOVESWEPT #436. Judy orchestrates perfectly this romance between Sharon Leslie, a gifted musician in whose heart the music has all but died, and Marc Duval, a man who's endured an unbearable tragedy and learned to find beauty and peace in the music he plays. Marc sees how Sharon is drawn to and yet tormented by the melodies he sends to her on the wind—as she is to his mesmerizing kisses. He knows she doubts herself as a woman even as he awakens her to pleasure beyond anything she's ever known. But until he can earn Sharon's trust, he can't know why she keeps turning away from him—and once she does trust him, he realizes he will have to confess the black secret of his own past. Caught up in the rebirth of the music inside her, Sharon revels in her feelings for Marc, but it all comes crashing down on her when she discovers the truth about the man she now loves with all her heart. Judy gives us a shining example of how true love conquers all in this wonderfully touching romance.

Fayrene Preston continues her SwanSea Place series with **JEOPARDY,** LOVESWEPT #437. Judging by the hero's name alone, Amarillo Smith, you can expect this to be one sultry, exciting, dangerous romance that only Fayrene can write—and you won't be disappointed. Heroine Angelica DiFrenza is surprised and intrigued when private investigator Amarillo, her brother's partner, asks her to dinner—the broodingly handsome detective had always seemed to avoid her deliberately. But when they finally end up alone together, the passion flares hotter than a blast furnace, and they both realize there's no going back. Amarillo couldn't deny

(continued)

what he'd felt for so long, but the time wasn't right. He was desperate to protect Angelica from the danger that threatened her life, and he needed a clear head and un-involved emotions to do it. But Amarillo's tantalizing kisses create a fever in Angelica's blood and the maelstrom of uncivilized hunger they'd suspected brewed between them rages out of control. You'll want to follow these two along on their journey of discovery, which, of course, leads them to beautiful SwanSea Place.

We promised you more information about our LOVESWEPT hotline, and here it is! If you'd like to reach your favorite LOVESWEPT authors by phone, all you have to do is dial 1-900-896-2505 between October 1 and December 31 to hear exciting mes-sages and up-to-the-minute information. You *may* call and get the author in person! Not only will you be able to get the latest news and gossip, but just by calling and leaving your name you will be entered into our Romantic Getaway Sweepstakes, where you'll have a chance to win a grand prize of a free week for two to Paris! Each call you make will cost you 95¢ per min-ute, and winners of the contest will be chosen at random from the names gathered. More detailed in-struction and rules will appear in the backs of our November, December, and January LOVESWEPTs. But the number will be operational beginning on October 1 and ending on December 31!

Get your dialing fingers ready!

Sincerely,

Susann Brailey

Susann Brailey
Editor
LOVESWEPT
Bantam Books
666 Fifth Avenue
New York, NY 10103

FOREVER LOVESWEPT

SPECIAL KEEPSAKE EDITION OFFER

$12.95

VALUE

Here's your chance to receive a special hardcover Loveswept "Keepsake Edition" to keep close to your heart forever. Collect hearts (shown on next page) found in the back of Loveswepts #426-#449 (on sale from September 1990 through December 1990). Once you have collected a total of 15 hearts, fill out the coupon and selection form on the next page (no photocopies or hand drawn facsimiles will be accepted) and mail to: Loveswept Keepsake, P.O. Box 9014, Bohemia, NY 11716.

FOREVER LOVESWEPT
SPECIAL KEEPSAKE EDITION OFFER
SELECTION FORM

Choose from these special Loveswepts by your favorite authors. Please write a 1 next to your first choice, a 2 next to your second choice. Loveswept will honor your preference as inventory allows.

♡   *Loveswept* ®

_____BAD FOR EACH OTHER   Billie Green

_____NOTORIOUS   Iris Johansen

_____WILD CHILD   Suzanne Forster

_____A WHOLE NEW LIGHT   Sandra Brown

_____HOT TOUCH   Deborah Smith

_____ONCE UPON A TIME...GOLDEN
        THREADS   Kay Hooper

Attached are 15 hearts and the selection form which indicates my choices for my special hardcover Loveswept "Keepsake Edition." Please mail my book to:

NAME:_____

ADDRESS:_____

CITY/STATE:_____ ZIP:_____

Offer open only to residents of the United States, Puerto Rico and Canada. Void where prohibited, taxed, or restricted. Allow 6 - 8 weeks after receipt of coupons for delivery. Offer expires January 15, 1991. You will receive your first choice as inventory allows; if that book is no longer available, you'll receive your second choice, etc.